Six winners. Six fantasies.

Six skeletons come out of the closet...

Plain Jane Kurtz is going to use her
winnings to discover her inner vixen.
But what's it *really* going to cost her?

New girl in town Nicole Reavis is on a journey
to find herself. But what *else* will she discover
along the way?

Risk taker Eve Best is on the verge of having
everything she's ever wanted.
But can she take it?

Young, cocky Zach Haas loves his instant
popularity, especially with the women.
But can he trust it?

Solid, dependable Cole Crawford
is ready to shake things up.
But how "shook up" is he prepared to handle?

Wild child Liza has always just wanted to belong.
But how far is she willing to go to get it?

Million Dollar Secrets—do you feel lucky?

Blaze™

Dear Reader,

Have you ever dreamed of winning the lottery? Jane Kurtz regularly plays the lottery with her coworkers, but she never really thinks about winning. Why would she? Everything in Jane's life is perfectly ordinary—her looks, her car, her life. When she overhears her hot next-door neighbor make a crack about her sad little life, she longs to do something completely wild and unexpected, and then...she and her coworkers have the winning ticket! Jane shocks everyone by going to Vegas for a wild weekend. But Jane herself is shocked when her hot neighbor follows her to make sure she doesn't get into trouble...with anyone but him!

I hope you enjoy this first of six books in the MILLION DOLLAR SECRETS miniseries. Please share with your friends the great stories that you read between the pages of Harlequin novels! Visit me at www.stephaniebond.com.

Much love and laughter,

Stephanie Bond

STEPHANIE BOND

*she did a bad,
bad thing*

HARLEQUIN®

TORONTO • NEW YORK • LONDON
AMSTERDAM • PARIS • SYDNEY • HAMBURG
STOCKHOLM • ATHENS • TOKYO • MILAN • MADRID
PRAGUE • WARSAW • BUDAPEST • AUCKLAND

ISBN-13: 978-0-373-79342-6
ISBN-10:   0-373-79342-1

SHE DID A BAD, BAD THING

ABOUT THE AUTHOR

Stephanie Bond feels she won the lottery in November 1995—when Harlequin bought her very first book! Since then, Stephanie has written over twenty-five books for Harlequin, and still loves bringing stories of romance and comedy to her readers all over the world. Stephanie lives in Atlanta, Georgia, with her husband, Christopher. She loves to hear from her readers at www.stephaniebond.com.

Books by Stephanie Bond

HARLEQUIN BLAZE
2—TWO SEXY!
169—MY FAVORITE MISTAKE
282—JUST DARE ME...

MIRA BOOKS
BODY MOVERS
BODY MOVERS: 2 BODIES FOR THE PRICE OF 1

HARLEQUIN TEMPTATION
685—MANHUNTING IN MISSISSIPPI
718—CLUB CUPID
751—ABOUT LAST NIGHT...
769—IT TAKES A REBEL
787—TOO HOT TO SLEEP
805—SEEKING SINGLE MALE
964—COVER ME

Don't miss any of our special offers. Write to us at the following address for information on our newest releases.

Harlequin Reader Service
U.S.: 3010 Walden Ave., P.O. Box 1325, Buffalo, NY 14269
Canadian: P.O. Box 609, Fort Erie, Ont. L2A 5X3

This book is dedicated to all my readers
who find the riches in their everyday lives
with family and friends.

1

"LISTEN…I'M sorry—what was your name again?"

Jane Kurtz turned off the handheld airbrush machine that was depositing a perfect layer of makeup over the zits of celebutante Casey Campella, today's guest on *Just Between Us*. "It's Jane."

"Oh…right." Casey wrinkled her nose. "Listen, I don't want to look orange on camera. I have a lot of friends and family here in Atlanta, and they'll all be watching the show."

Watching for tips on how to make their own home sex tape reminiscent of the one of Casey and her current boyfriend that was making the rounds on the Internet. Jane bit her tongue to keep from saying that as far as Casey appearing on camera looking too orange was concerned, it was too late.

Instead Jane wet her lips. "I promise you

won't look orange, Ms. Campella. But I'm afraid you'll have to be still in order for me to do the best job possible."

Casey sniffed and looked away.

Jane turned the airbrush machine on again and continued to apply a flawless application of makeup on the young woman's face, conceding that what she lacked in skin texture, she made up for in bone structure. The only thing higher than the woman's cheekbones were her boobs, which allegedly had their own fan club *and* Website.

When the foundation layer was complete, Jane turned off the machine and proceeded to enhance the woman's deep blue eyes with strategic applications of false eyelashes, highlighters, shadows, and liner.

Next came the cheeks, which needed only a touch of sparkle, then the biggest challenge—creating the illusion of a pouty, well-defined mouth from pencil-thin lips in a shade of red that would make the woman's nicotine-stained teeth look as white as possible. All this while Casey talked on her phone with her boyfriend, who, from the one-sided R-rated conversation, appeared to be as immature as the giggling starlet—and very possible masturbating on the other end.

"I had a dream about you last night, baby…no, me first…no, me first…okay, you go ahead…oh, baby-cakes, that's so hot I can hardly stand it…uh-huh…I want you so bad right now…."

In the midst of her frustration and embarrassment, Jane tamped down a stab of jealousy. What would it be like to have a man so crazy for you that he called you up to say naughty things?

"Five minutes," an associate producer cued from the doorway, and Casey indicated that she'd heard.

"Gotta run, baby. Be sure to tape the show… we'll watch it together." From her throaty laugh, it was clear what they planned to do while they watched her discuss their sex life on the hottest regional talk show around.

Fighting an eye roll, Jane sensed another sex tape in the making.

Casey disconnected the call, then leaned forward in the bright illumination of the mirror to scrutinize her makeup from every angle. Her forehead furrowed in a frown.

"Is there a problem, Ms. Campella?" Jane asked.

"No. In fact, I look…amazing."

Jane smiled and gave a little nod. "I'm glad you're pleased."

"Thank you, uh—what was your name again?"

"Jane."

"Right." Casey stood and tore off the paper cape protecting the red trench-coat style mini-dress that Jane had chosen for her from wardrobe. It struck the perfect balance between classy and trashy. The curvy celebrity did a twirl in the full-length mirror, winked at herself, then looked Jane up and down. "I'm just wondering, if you can make other people look this good, why don't you do something for yourself?"

Jane's smile dissolved as the woman strode away in the decadent Donald Pliner black stiletto boots that Jane had spent the better part of two days hunting down. A few seconds later, music sounded and the audience burst into wild applause and cheers, indicating that the current "it" girl had blessed them with her appearance.

In a spin that only host Eve Best could put on the eyebrow-raising topic, this episode, she claimed, was for women who wanted to add a little spice to their marriage. To hear Eve tell it, revealing the DOs and DON'Ts of making an at-home sex tape was practically a public service for housewives.

Jane shook her head and expelled a little laugh as she watched the monitor overhead. With the host of the show and today's guest both looking better than nature intended, her workday was essentially over, although, officially she stayed until the show signed off in the event of a shine-blotting emergency.

She carefully cleaned all the tools and containers she used to cleanse, moisturize, exfoliate, shave and tweeze, plus the appliances to apply makeup and false eyelashes and to fill in the occasional over-plucked eyebrow. As her hands moved automatically, performing the job she'd performed every day for the past three years, her mind wandered back to Casey Campella's cutting remark.

Jane glanced into the mirror that was her customary work environment and acknowledged ruefully that the bouncy celebrity had only voiced what every other person whom Jane worked on probably wondered:

How could a talented and sought-after makeup artist and stylist be so unattractive?

For the most part, Jane avoided mirrors. When she brushed her teeth, for instance, she didn't stop to analyze the ordinary placement of her unremarkable features—the common pale blue eyes, the standard eyebrows, the average nose, the regular mouth, the unexceptional skin tone, all framed by run of the mill light brown hair of middling length.

All in all, an extremely forgettable face.

She hadn't been blessed with the natural good looks of her two childhood friends Eve Best and Liza Skinner. Over the years, Jane had settled into her role, living up to the nickname of Plain Jane. She preferred blue jeans and Merrills to dresses and Manolos.

But Jane had enjoyed it when her friends played dress-up, had delighted in using cosmetics to make them even more beautiful. By the time they all were in high school, she was doing their makeup every morning in the girls' restroom. Jane discovered she had a keen eye for camouflaging flaws and highlighting assets…in others' faces. The few times she had experimented on her own face had been dismal failures—she had looked as if she were trying too hard to be pretty…as if she were trying to compete with her friends.

Making other people look good had become second nature…and in some cases, her plainness helped those under her ministrations to relax. Most celebrities were so insecure about their flaws, the last thing they wanted was to be at the mercy of a makeup artist who was prettier.

Her plainness had become her trademark, she reminded herself. She had taken the mediocre hand that life that dealt her and bluffed her way to an enviable job…a job that some might even call glamorous, although when Eve had first asked her to come on board, it had been a risk. In the beginning, she and Liza both had done whatever it took to get the show on the air, even if it fell outside their job description. But over the years the skeletal staff had grown to more than forty technicians, office and production staff, and station executives. Now Jane could concentrate on being the show's stylist and makeup artist. It was challenging and rewarding. It allowed her to rub elbows with the rich and famous. It made up for the social life she didn't have.

When the pep-talk smile she gave to herself in the mirror fell short of convincing, Jane simply looked away.

While she sterilized every brush and applicator, she watched the television monitor, pleased that both Eve and her guest looked great from every camera angle—somewhere between radiant and matte under the glare of the hot lamps of the set lights.

"So, Casey," Eve said with the solemnity of someone who was interviewing a political candidate, "what should our viewers know about making their own intimacy video at home?"

It was just the kind of scintillating topic that had increased the show's viewership by leaps and bounds over the past three years. *Just Between Us* was now commanding high advertising rates. A feature piece in a national media magazine had put the talk show and Eve on the radar of the major networks. The energy level on the set had increased—along with the pressure to deliver. Everyone seemed on edge lately.

Jane dropped a tray of makeup samples.

Including her.

She crouched to clean up the mess, chastising herself for her clumsiness. It was the uncertainty of the show's future, she reasoned, that was making her feel so…restless. It had nothing to do with the fact that she seemed destined to stay under life's radar. People couldn't even remember her name.

Jane watched Eve work her magic on the unwitting guest and audience and wondered idly if Liza was keeping tabs on the show wherever she was. Flamboyant and volatile Liza Skinner had been the show's first story producer and was responsible for some of their most successful segments. But a year ago a disagreement over a segment that had gone badly had led to Liza blowing up and walking out on the show. They hadn't heard from her since. Jane missed her and knew that Eve did, too. And deep down, they both expected Liza to reappear one morning in her office and pick up where she'd left off as if nothing had happened.

Jane thought of her every time they took up money for the Lot O' Bucks lottery—pooling their money for tickets was a tradition that she and Eve and Liza had started, with each of them choosing two of the six numbers. Since Liza had left, three other employees had joined the pool and contributed what they hoped would be a winning number, but she and Eve had stubbornly held on to one of Liza's numbers as a gesture of their friendship. They had joked it was like leaving a light in the window. Meanwhile, Jane hoped that their friend was safe.

By the time she stored her tools in their proper places, the show had ended and the director was giving everyone on the set a thumbs-up.

Jane turned down the monitor and took inventory of the shades of foundation, eye, cheek, and lip color. She noted which rows were running low and phoned in replacements orders. Then she did a quick survey of the clothing racks and made a few notes on new spring accessories she wanted to add. From her mail crate, she opened and sorted through dozens of sample products and catalogs that had been sent to her from various manufacturers and retailers. The promising ones went into a large canvas tote for closer scrutiny in her home office.

When she stepped out into the hall, she smiled at Eve who was striding her way. "Great show."

Eve grinned. "Thanks. I was a little nervous about how Casey would come across, but she did a good job. And her makeup and outfit were perfect, thanks to you. She looked downright credible."

"Good."

"But you have your work cut out for you tomorrow. Bette Valentine with the unibrow will be here to talk about unleashing your inner wild child."

Jane winced. "And those muu-muus she wears are hard to do anything with."

"You'll think of something," Eve said with a wink. "Do you have a hot date tonight?"

"Yeah—with my remote control." The season finale of her favorite show, *Dirty Secrets of Daylily Drive,* aired tonight. She was eager to see who had murdered the neighborhood bimbo.

Eve made a rueful noise. "When are you going to start dating again? It's been months since you and James called it quits."

Since he dumped me, Jane corrected silently. And although she acknowledged that James wasn't the love of her life, his parting remark still cut to the bone. *Gawd, Jane, you're such a bore.* His offhand slight had sent her into a funk that she hadn't yet recovered from. Her cheeks still burned when she relived the memory.

"I don't have time to date," she said, then smirked. "Maybe I should talk to my boss about cutting back my hours."

"Touché. As soon as we go nationwide," Eve said, linking her arm with Jane's and walking with her to the exit, "we'll both get a life." Suddenly a serious expression crossed Eve's face. "You haven't heard from Liza, have you?"

"No, why?"

"No reason, really. She's just been on my mind today."

"Mine, too," Jane admitted. "Wonder where she is?"

Eve shook her head. "Knowing Liza, she could be on the moon." She waved. "See you tomorrow."

Jane waved and watched her friend walk away. Eve, she knew, still had hours of work ahead of her before she could leave the station.

Eve Best deserved to make it big—the woman worked twice as hard as anyone else on the show. Even when they were young, Jane had the feeling that her two friends were destined for great things.

Then Jane worried her lower lip with her teeth. Maybe this emotional slump was simply a phase she was going through. But with Liza gone, she couldn't help but feel that the big break they were all waiting for would only tear them further apart...

2

PUSHING ASIDE THE troubling premonition, Jane left the station and climbed into her old but trusty Civic. Dusk was falling on the chilly spring day and fatigue pulled at her shoulders as she pointed her car in the direction of her condo. On normal days, the commute was manageable—a miracle by Atlanta traffic standards. But today she was behind a minor accident and construction backup on Peachtree Street. At the last minute, she decided to veer off to pick up Chinese food in lieu of cooking. It was already dark by the time she pulled into the parking garage for her building.

When she rounded the corner to her assigned parking spot, she bit back a curse—a little red sports car occupied her place, next to an enormous black SUV that belonged to her new neighbor. She hadn't yet met him, but she'd heard him moving in yesterday and hoped that he would be settled by tonight. Indeed, it appeared that he already had a guest over and was already violating the building rules. She resented the people who thought living in a condo was like living in an apartment—the man was a home-owner and he'd better start acting like it. Fuming, she parked in the cramped guest parking area and headed inside.

The sooner he was indoctrinated to the rules of condo living, the better.

She stopped in front of her neighbor's door and juggled her shoulder bag, an armload of catalogs, and the bag of Chinese takeout to ring the doorbell. From behind the door she heard music pulsing with a throbbing bass. She rang the doorbell again and after several long minutes, the door swung open.

The angry words at the back of her throat dissolved.

The man stood well over six feet tall. His hair and eyes were dark, and his jaw sported a couple of days' worth of scruff. His skin was golden brown, and since he wore only faded jeans, she could see a lot of it. His shoulders were wide and muscled, his chest covered with a mat of black hair that disappeared into the waistband slung low enough to make her wonder if he wore any under-wear. From the way he held his long body to the magnetism that rolled off him like a natural cologne, the man appeared to be built for sex.

In a word, he was devastating.

He appeared to be studying her, too, but from the way he tipped up his bottle of beer, he appar-ently found her slightly less noteworthy. "Can I help you?" he drawled.

"Uh…I'm your next door neighbor. Jane."

He nodded and flashed a killer smile. "I'm Perry. Nice to meet you."

"Same here." She shifted the precarious load in her arms and decided against extending her hand. "Do you drive a black SUV?"

"Yeah."

"There's a red car next to it in my parking spot. I thought you might know who it belongs to."

"Kayla," he yelled over his shoulder, then took a pull on his beer.

A lush brunette appeared, impossibly tiny and curvy in a Barbie Doll kind of way and sporting a midriff revealing sweater. For some ridiculous reason, Jane was disappointed in the man's taste, but then what had she expected?

"What, baby?" the girl crooned.

"Did you park in guest parking like I told you?"

She pouted. "The spots were too close together—I didn't want my car to get dinged, so I parked next to your SUV."

He looked at Jane and shrugged apologetically. "Sorry, uh—what did you say your name was?"

"Jane," she said through gritted teeth.

He pointed his finger like a gun and made a clicking noise. "Won't happen again."

She opened her mouth to ask that his guest move her car, but the door closed in her face. Jane scowled, hoping the man—to paraphrase Jane Austen—improved upon closer acquaintance. The building housed only forty condos. A few jerks— or one large one—would be enough to cause problems for everyone. And since she and Perry shared a wall and a divided balcony, she would bear the brunt of it.

Heaving a sigh, she unlocked the door to her own condo. Inside, she dropped her load on her desk, then carried the bag of Chinese food to the living room, turning on lights along the way.

The sight of her condo never failed to calm her—she'd purposely decorated in a minimalist style in soothing shades of taupe and sky blue to make the space her own personal haven. Her walls were white, her furniture streamlined. No clutter to distract her, no mess to create more work when she should be winding down.

Jane sighed and felt the stress of the day drain away. She changed into comfy sweats and pulled her hair back into a ponytail. A glance at the clock had her rushing to the kitchen for a bottle of water and a TV tray. Time for her show. Guilty pleasure filled her chest—would Victoria and the cop Nate get together? Or would Nate arrest Victoria for murdering her neighbor?

Settling onto her overstuffed couch, Jane

slipped off her shoes and dug her toes into the plush area rug, then clicked on the TV and reached for the bag of takeout. Suddenly the blare of pulsing music invaded her space.

Jane frowned in the direction of the shared wall. The previous owner had been quiet—and had traveled often. Hopefully her new neighbor would soon realize that the walls of multi-family-unit buildings could be thin.

Tamping down irritation, she increased the volume of the TV to counter the sound of the music coming through the wall. From the bag she removed a container of crab wontons and another of lo mein.

She unwrapped the chopsticks and had a wonton halfway to her mouth when the sound of a woman's voice came through the wall.

"Ahh…ahh, yeah, baby, that's it…yeah."

Jane stopped and turned her head toward the wall. It wasn't…they weren't…

Incredulous, she lowered the volume on the television, only to be treated to a new string of sexpletives.

"Oh, oh, oh…yes! Yes! Do it! Harder! Faster! I-eeeee! Omigod, omigod, omigod, that feels so good! Talk dirty to me—yeah, that's it…you nasty, nasty boy."

Jane's eyes widened. Nasty boy?

A rhythmic banging sounded on the wall and she thought at first that one of them was hitting the wall with a wayward limb…then she realized with the accompanying squeaking noises that it was the man's headboard that was banging against their shared wall.

"Oh, good grief," she muttered, feeling a little dirty, like a voyeur, yet curiously unable to stop listening. The woman's caterwauling escalated in time with the banging noise and was joined by a man's low voice.

"Now!" she screamed. "I'm coming! Now! Now! NOWWWW!"

From the synchronized clamor, it appeared that they arrived together. Jane sat unmoving, unable to believe what had just transpired, but distantly aware of a heaviness in her breasts and a tingle of desire in her midsection.

Embarrassment swelled in her chest and she grappled with the remote to increase the volume over the music still pounding through the wall. She tried to concentrate on the storyline of the show, but her mind kept returning to the fact that she'd just heard her new neighbor have sex.

As far as neighbors went, that fell under the category of TMI: Too Much Information. Especially since she could visualize his long, muscular body naked and sweaty, tangled in the sheets... And she wondered what kind of nasty things he'd said to the woman that had made her scream as if she'd hung between life and death.

Working her mouth back and forth, Jane studied a crab wonton, then popped it into her mouth. It was the most satisfying thing *she* would get tonight.

But as her attention continued to wander and she realized that she'd missed huge chunks of the program, her irritation ballooned again. Nasty Boy had foisted his sex life on her and completely ruined her evening. And while she stewed about the man's crudeness—and rudeness—the rhythmic thumping started up again along with the woman's commentary.

"Oh, baby, that's it...that's it...oh, yeah. Say something nasty...oh, yeah."

Jane stuck her tongue into her cheek. Not again. She hadn't even had time to finish her dinner! Worse, she had no idea what was happening on her show.

She stabbed at the lo mein as the movement on the other side of the wall grew more frenetic. Nasty Boy apparently had stamina...and finesse. He knew just where to put it, oh baby, he knew just how to do it, oh yeah.

It was like bad song lyrics.

What was he saying to her? She leaned closer to the wall, but couldn't make out the low murmurings. With a jolt, Jane realized that she was rocking in time with the couples' rhythm and she was feeling...warm.

And...moist.

How long had it been since she'd had sex? There hadn't been anyone since James, and the last few times with him had been a letdown.

Who was she kidding? *Every* time with James had been a letdown. Every time with every guy— not that there'd been that many—had been a letdown. None of her encounters with men had lived up to the fantasies she'd spun in her head, not one of them had left her feeling like this…with desire coiled tightly in her stomach, aching for release.

Meanwhile, next door, the woman let go with the intensity and the volume of a hurricane, screeching and banging in a clatter that grated on Jane's nerves like a fire alarm sounding. Unreasonable anger rose in her chest and she pushed to her feet. She would *not* be subjected to this kind of…*exhibitionism* in her own home!

Striding out into the hallway, she knocked loudly on Perry's door, and when he didn't answer, she knocked again, her ire rising even higher. She had lifted her arm to bang on his door again when it suddenly swung open, revealing her neighbor in his long glory, his hair tousled and wearing the jeans that now were only half-zipped. And she had the feeling that this time, he definitely wasn't wearing underwear.

He gave her a lopsided smile.. "Can I help you, uh…what was your name again?"

"Jane," she snapped.

"Right. What can I do for you?"

"You can take it down a notch."

"What do you mean?"

"I mean that you and I share a wall and I can hear your…music."

"Okay, I'll turn down the volume on the stereo." He started to close the door, but she held up her hand. Knowing what he'd done to generate the sheen of perspiration on his chest threatened to tie her tongue in knots, but she reminded herself that she was the victim here. "I can also hear your, um…activities."

He blinked. "Activities?"

She crossed her arms and gave him a pointed look. "Both times."

His dark eyebrows shot up, then a devilish smile curved his mouth. "And on a scale of one to ten?"

She gasped, outraged. "I didn't come over to *score* you, Mr.—"

"Brewer," he supplied.

Her mouth tightened. "Mr. Brewer, I came over to ask you as a neighbor to please keep the noise down."

"I'll try," he said cheerfully, "but I can't make any promises." Then he stepped back and closed the door.

Jane stood there for a few seconds, feeling like a fool. She slunk back to her condo, furious to see that her show had ended, then paced the living room with pent-up energy. To escape, she poured herself a glass of wine and went out to sit on her tiny balcony that faced west, overlooking the lights of Midtown.

Adrenaline coursed through her body—anger, embarrassment, frustration. She felt as if she were coming out of her skin, and couldn't rightly blame all of it on her neighbor's unwitting intrusion. Maybe she was coming down with something… maybe she was experiencing some sort of chemical imbalance. That would explain this profound restlessness that, in truth, had preceded her breakup with James, but had escalated afterward. She had the strangest sensation that her life was careening downhill, picking up speed, but headed nowhere. It wasn't anything she could put her finger on, just a feeling of being...unfulfilled.

When she heard the slide of her neighbor's balcony door opening, her heart sank—with him permeating her living space, her balcony was her last sanctuary. A tall concrete wall separated their balconies, but that wouldn't keep her from hearing their call of the wild should they decide to move their gymnastics outdoors. She braced herself for more lewd noises.

Instead, the woman's high-pitched laugh reached her ears. "I can't believe your nerdy neighbor came over to tell you that she heard us having sex through the walls. How rude!"

Brewer's laugh was short. "More like a prude."

Heat rose in Jane's face and she sank lower in her chair.

"Maybe you should find someplace else to live," his partner suggested, then she laughed. "Because we're going to drive her crazy. And then, she's going to drive *you* crazy."

"Why should I leave?" Brewer said. "Because I had the misfortune of moving in next to a homely little geek who's probably never had a good lay and has nothing better to do than listen to other people get it on?"

Jane inhaled sharply against the pain in her chest. Her skin burned with needles of humiliation…is that how other people saw her? Emotion clogged her throat and tears pricked her eyes. She stood up abruptly, distantly registering the fact that she'd dropped her wine glass, but not caring as she fled inside.

PERRY HEARD the sound of glass crashing on the other side of the balcony wall. He winced, realizing that his neighbor—Jane, wasn't it?—had been sitting on the other side and had very likely heard what he'd said. *Damn*.

"What was that?" Kayla asked.

"Nothing," he said, feeling like a heel as he lifted his beer to drain it. "Maybe you should go— I have to be in court in the morning and I still have some files to go through."

Kayla pouted. "Okay. When will I see you again?"

"Soon," he promised, escorting her back inside

and toward the door. He lowered a perfunctory kiss on her mouth, and shepherded her out into the hall, sending her off with a wave.

Then he paused and looked at his neighbor's door, wondering if he should apologize, how he *could* apologize for calling her a… He squinted to remember.

A homely little geek who's probably never had a good lay.

He cringed, thinking that no matter how mousy the woman was, she didn't deserve that kind of put-down. His mother had raised him better than that.

Perry pulled on his chin and vowed to find a way to make it up to Jane what's-her-name…somehow.

3

THE NEXT MORNING, Jane stepped out into the hallway and set down a bag of garbage so she could lock her condo door. She blinked rapidly to focus on the lock through the sunglasses—ridiculous, but necessary to hide her gritty, puffy eyes. Her new neighbor and his girlfriend would get a good belly laugh if they knew that their offhand remarks about her sad little life had caused her a sleepless night of crying into her pillow. She was quite sure she was so insignificant to them that they wouldn't even recall what they'd said.

While she struggled to slide the key into the keyhole, her new neighbor's door opened, to her dismay. She didn't look up, just stabbed at the keyhole as a flush raced up her neck and face.

"Good morning," he said.

"Morning," she murmured, keeping her back to him.

"Having problems?"

"No." She set her jaw and tried to steady her hand, but she continued to fumble.

Suddenly a large hand closed over hers gently. "Let me."

She stiffened, but relinquished the key and stepped back from his big body just to escape his touch. She turned, expecting to see his girlfriend loitering nearby, but he was alone, and dressed in a suit as best as she could tell through her dark lenses. His briefcase sat on the floor next to her garbage bag.

The deadbolt clicked. Then he turned and handed her the keys, flashing a smile.

"Thanks," she muttered.

"Hey, no wonder you couldn't see," he said with a laugh. "What's up with the shades?"

And before she realized what he was doing, he had lifted them from her face. She blinked at the sudden light and grabbed to retrieve the glasses, mortified for him to see her swollen, red-rimmed eyes. If he thought she was homely yesterday, this morning she was downright ugly.

She saw him blanch before she jammed the dark glasses back on her face. "Allergies," she murmured, then reached for her garbage.

"I got that," he said, snatching up the bag. "Actually, you can show me where I need to put my trash."

She didn't say anything, just nodded, and walked down the hall to the garbage chute. "There," she said, pointing. "See you later."

She veered off toward the stairs, thinking he'd take the elevator. Instead, after dropping the garbage, he followed her down the stairs.

"Hey, I'm sorry again about the noise last night," he said. "I didn't realize the walls were so thin."

She didn't respond—she knew Perry Brewer's type. He'd throw a few nice words her way, then ask her to be home to sign for his furniture delivery. Jane picked up the pace and managed to reach the parking garage first.

"I didn't get your last name," he said a few paces behind her.

She rolled her eyes—as if he remembered her *first* name.

He caught up to her and gave her a little smile. "Come on, we're neighbors—I should know your last name."

"It's Kurtz. Goodbye." She strode past her empty parking spot toward the guest parking area, relieved to be away from him, although she could feel his gaze boring into her back, surveying her chinos, yellow polo shirt, black Skechers sneakers and ponytail. Was he fascinated in her as a geeky specimen?

When she reached her car, she groaned to see a sizable dent in her driver's side door, obviously caused by the door of another car that was long gone. She removed her dark glasses and bent to run her hand over the dent—her car was old, but she tried to take good care of it. To add insult to injury, she realized suddenly that her back tire was flat, caused, no doubt, by the nail sticking out of it. A handful of nails lay scattered around the back of her car, probably dropped by some maintenance worker who also parked in the guest area.

She blinked back hot tears—she didn't need

this. She'd overslept because she was so tired and was already running late.

At the sound of a car slowing, she turned her head to see the big, black SUV, and Perry leaning toward the lowered passenger side window. "Need a ride?"

She wiped her eyes and jammed the glasses back on her face. "No, I'll call a repair service."

"That could take a while. I can drop you wherever you need to be."

She massaged her temples—she just wanted the vile man to go away.

"I feel responsible," he called, then leaned over and opened the passenger side door. "Let me do this."

Jane stared at the open door. Then she glanced at her watch. It would mean the difference between her getting to work on time or throwing her entire day—and maybe the show—off schedule.

"Come on," he cajoled. Jane decided it was the least he could do since his girlfriend was the root cause of her current predicament.

She walked over and took the hand he extended to climb into the SUV. His fingers were strong and warm as they enclosed hers. She clambered into the seat with an unladylike bounce, and tugged her hand from his. She closed the door and sat as close to it as possible while she put on her seatbelt. Perry was smiling at her like some kind of gallant knight in training. Even through the dark glasses, she could see he was more handsome in his suit than he'd been half-dressed last night. And she was surprised to discover that Nasty Boy had a professional job.

"Where am I taking you?" he asked.

She tore her gaze from him to stare straight ahead and gave him the street address.

"That's the cable TV station, isn't it?"

She nodded.

"What do you do for them?"

Jane squirmed, reluctant to give the man any more ammunition to use against her.

"I work on a local talk show."

"What's the name of the show?"

"Just Between Us."

"Hey, that's the show with the looker host, right?"

"Eve Best...yes, she's beautiful." Jane looked

out the window, with the words that he'd said about her own appearance looping in her head. *Homely little geek...homely little geek...homely little geek.* She inched closer to the door.

"Sounds like an exciting job," he said, but she didn't offer any commentary. The silence stretched awkwardly, and she willed the morning traffic to move faster.

His cell phone rang and he said, "Excuse me," then hit a hands-free speaker button on his visor. "Perry Brewer."

"You're late," a woman's voice accused.

"Good morning to you, too, Theresa. I'm on my way."

"You're due in court in thirty minutes, cowboy. Are you going to make it?"

"I'll be there," he said smoothly. "And I have the files I need."

"I don't have to tell you what's riding on this hearing, Perry."

"No, Theresa, you don't," he said, his voice more solemn.

"Good luck. Call me when it's over."

"Will do." He disconnected the call, then glanced over at Jane. "Sorry about that."

"No problem," she said. "But it sounds as if I'm making you late. You can let me out here and I'll get a taxi."

"No need," he said easily. "We're almost there, and I'll be going against traffic when I leave your office."

Silence fell between them again, and Jane started to feel rude for not reciprocating his small talk. "So you're an attorney?"

He cracked a little smile. "That's what my business card says."

"And you have a big case today?"

"Bigger than most."

She pictured him in front of a courtroom and realized that the man was probably good at what he did—he was, after all, charming, convincing…two-faced.

With the requisite small talk out of the way, she concentrated on the bumper of the car in front of them, checked the strap on her shoulder bag and generally fidgeted. The man made her nervous and hyperaware of her appearance. Next to his ultra-feminine girlfriend, she felt like a boy.

And she didn't like it.

PERRY WATCHED the slender woman next to him out of the corner of his eye, squirming, positioning herself as far away from him as possible. He felt like a jerk. Seeing those puffy eyes of hers this morning was like a punch to his gut—it didn't take a genius to figure out that his callous words of the night before had upset her…had made her cry all night from the looks of it.

He tightened his grip on the steering wheel, remorse coursing through him. Words of apology watered in his mouth, but he had a feeling that he'd only make things worse if he brought it up. Still, he had to own up to his bad behavior.

"Listen…Jane," he said, choosing his words carefully. "I have a big mouth and I have a feeling that you overheard something I said last night that…was unkind."

She didn't say anything, but he could tell by the way she stiffened that he was right—she had overheard him…and her red-rimmed eyes had nothing to do with allergies.

"I'm sorry," he said quietly.

"No need to apologize," she said quickly, tugging on the strap of her bag. "You have a right to your opinion."

"But I didn't mean it. I was in a bad mood and I'd had too much to drink."

She gave him a little half smile. "It's okay, Mr. Brewer—I have a mirror. I know that I'm not… exciting."

The resignation in her voice tugged at his heart. "Jane—"

"That's my building on the corner. I'll get out here."

"I'll drive you to the front—"

But she was already out of the vehicle, swinging down to the curb.

"Do you need a ride home?" he shouted, strangely eager to do something else for her.

"No, thanks. Good luck on your case." Then she slammed the door and took off jogging toward the entrance of her building.

He watched her moving away from him, juggling her oversized shoulder bag, her ponytail bouncing like a teenager's. Dressed like a coed, she looked young…and alone. And she had wished him luck on his case…even after what he'd said about her, she had tried to be nice.

Were there really people like that left in the world?

A horn sounded behind him, jarring him out of his reverie. He hit the gas pedal and told himself to focus—he was facing the biggest case of his career this morning.

Yet all he could think about on the way to the courthouse was the young woman he had wounded with his careless words. And he realized with a start that he'd like to get to know Jane Kurtz better…if only he could convince her to let him.

4

Jane's skin tingled with humiliation as she hurried to her office. She wasn't sure what was worse—knowing what Perry had said about her, or him knowing that she knew.

And him knowing that his words had affected her.

One thing was certain, she realized when she removed her sunglasses in the makeup room and got a good look at her red, swollen eyes—she was going to have to call upon some major concealer today, or she would spend the day fending off questions from her coworkers.

So she sat down in front of a brightly lit mirror and for the first time in a long time, began to apply some of her expertise to her own face. With a practiced eye, she dipped a sponge into a pot of foundation that was a shade lighter than her skin tone, and proceeded to erase the damage of the night's tears…if only it were so easy to erase the damage of his words cutting into her soul. His apology had only driven the knife deeper.

Worse, she couldn't figure out why she had let his words get to her. Because they had so directly fed into her own restlessness of late? Because she was worried that she was doomed to be ignored by everyone around her? To be alone indefinitely.

The appearance of her friend Eve Best for her daily makeup application ended Jane's musings. "Good morning!"

Eve was the most upbeat person Jane knew—just being around her made Jane feel better. "Good morning."

"Ready for me?"

"Sure." Jane stood and gestured toward the chair she'd vacated.

"How was your evening with your remote control?" Eve teased as she sat down.

"Interrupted," Jane said, shaking out a paper cape to tuck around the collar of Eve's blouse. "My new neighbor is so loud, he disturbed my entire evening."

"He?" Eve asked with a smile. "Have you met him?"

"Yes. Once to tell him that his girlfriend was parked in my parking place, and once to tell him to keep the noise down. And...I had a flat tire this morning, so he dropped me off here."

Eve's eyebrows rose. "Is he cute?"

Jane shrugged. "I guess so. But he's also a jerk."

"Gee, he can't be too much of a jerk if he offered you a ride to work."

Jane avoided Eve's perceptive gaze and instead handed her a headband to secure her hair away from her face. "How were ratings yesterday?" she asked, to change the subject.

Eve studied her with a little frown, then said, "The best ever. I need for today's show to be strong, too, to keep the viewers we captured yesterday."

"You'll pull it off," Jane said, hoping to soothe the concern she heard in her friend's voice.

Eve smiled at her in the mirror. "Thanks. But lately I've been asking myself why I'm doing this." She gave a little laugh. "My life would be so much easier if I could just win the lottery."

Jane laughed. "Mine, too." She checked the date on her watch. "Hey, maybe we'll get lucky today." She proceeded to airbrush a layer of foundation on Eve's lovely face, but this morning Jane's focus was compromised as she continually blinked her scratchy, sleep-deprived eyes. More than once she had to switch off the machine and correct mistakes manually.

"You okay?" Eve asked suspiciously. "You look tired."

"I…didn't get much sleep last night."

"Your neighbor again?"

Jane simply nodded, but spared her friend the gory details.

"Sounds like a fun guy," Eve said slyly.

Jane didn't respond, but admitted to herself that some of her tears last night had been due to the fact that Perry Brewer was correct in his assessment of her. Not only was she a homely geek, but listening to him pleasure his girlfriend had struck a chord in her—no man had ever given her that kind of physical satisfaction.

He was right. She'd never had a good lay in her life.

"Uh...Jane? Since when do you use green blush?"

Jane gasped at her ghoulish handiwork. "I'm sorry—I'll fix it."

"That neighbor of yours sure has you distracted," Eve remarked.

"Nothing a pair of earplugs won't fix," Jane murmured.

Turning her mind firmly away from Perry Brewer and his correct assumptions, she focused on Eve's makeup and methodically played up the woman's eyes, cheeks, and mouth. When she finished, Jane styled Eve's luxurious hair while they chatted about today's show.

"I just hope that 'Unleashing Your Inner Wild Child' appeals to enough viewers," Eve said wryly. "It sounds a little like a sexual exorcism."

Jane laughed and removed the paper cape, then stepped back and surveyed Eve's turquoise-colored blouse. "I have a necklace that would look great with that outfit."

From the bureau where she kept stock costume pieces, Jane removed a chunky silver and turquoise necklace and clasped it around Eve's neck. Eve touched the piece and smiled wide. "It's perfect. You have such a good eye, Jane."

Jane smiled. "That's what you pay me for."

An assistant producer appeared in the doorway. "Bette Valentine is here."

Eve glanced up at Jane. "And you're going to earn your paycheck today."

The women shared a laugh, then Eve heaved a sigh and pushed to her feet. "See you later."

"Okay," Jane said, fighting a yawn.

She had just finished cleaning up the vanity area when Bette Valentine sailed into the room sporting her typical tropical muu-muu, garish makeup, clanging earrings, and teased red hair.

"Hello, hello," the middle-aged woman sang.

"Hello, Ms. Valentine," Jane said, hoping her smile was stronger than it felt. "I'm Jane."

"I remember from the last time I was on the show," the woman said with a smile. "Although

I'm not sure why they sent me in here. I did my own makeup already."

"I'll just give you a little touch up," Jane said, gesturing to the chair. "You don't want to look shiny under all those lights."

The woman sat down, her bracelets and other jewelry jangling.

"Ms. Valentine, just between us, you might want to remove any jewelry that makes noise. The microphone will pick it up and our viewers won't be able to hear you."

"Oh? We wouldn't want that," the woman conceded.

"And I think I have a color of eye shadow that will better highlight those gorgeous green eyes of yours."

One compliment at a time, she tweaked the woman's appearance to tone down the makeup, extract some poof from the hair, and she even found a silver beaded tassel belt to cinch the voluminous muu-muu.

"That's nice," the woman agreed with a nod. Then she angled her head at Jane. "You're quite pretty, you know."

Jane blanched, her tongue tied as her mind replayed her neighbor's brutal assessment of her. "No...I'm not."

Ms. Valentine laughed and gripped Jane's hands. "Dear, you're just the sort of person I'm targeting today. You need to 'Unleash your inner wild child.' "

A flush climbed Jane's neck. "I don't have...I mean, I'm not—"

"Do you have a man in your life, Jane?"

"No, but—"

"It's because you haven't released the passion that lives deep within you."

Jane squirmed. All this touchy-feely stuff made her nervous.

The woman clasped her hands tighter. "You have a secret. You hide behind your plain clothes and your ponytail because you're afraid to let men see the wild child in you that's dying to get out. Yet you grow bored with the men who don't recognize that about you."

Jane started to protest, but Bette stared into her eyes with such intensity that for a split second, Jane felt as if the woman had a "third eye," that she could see something that Jane herself couldn't even see.

"She's in there," Bette said, releasing one of Jane's hands and tapping her lightly on the chest. "You need to find the courage to unleash her."

Jane's heart was hammering beneath the woman's hand, and she couldn't speak—wouldn't know what to say if she could. For some reason, the woman's words made her want to laugh...and cry. It was as if she had channeled into Jane's deepest fear lately—that she was doomed to be the girl whose name no one could remember.

"Ms. Valentine," an assistant said from the door, "you're on in five."

The woman gave Jane's hand one last squeeze. "This one's for you, hon."

Jane simply stared after the flamboyant woman, feeling as if she'd been emotionally dive-bombed and blaming some of her vulnerability on her lack of sleep. But as she cleaned her tools and supplies, she turned up the monitor and watched the show with more interest than usual.

Eve introduced Bette Valentine to much applause—the colorful woman was a favorite guest. "Tell us what you mean, Bette, when you say that women should unleash their inner wild child."

Bette's voice was hypnotic and she emphasized main points with her elegant hands. "Women are taught from a young age to repress behavior that might seem unladylike or too aggressive, especially when it comes to sex. Some women internalize those behaviors to the point of extreme shyness, but inside, they're dying to burst out."

"And these are women we know?" Eve asked.

"Absolutely. Sometimes women whom you would least suspect. The facade they exhibit to the world is one of good-girl obedience, sometimes even submission. They are what everyone around them expects them to be." Bette leaned in conspiratorially. "But these women have a secret. Deep down, they're unhappy because they have this longing buried inside to do something wild, something completely unexpected to prove to themselves and to everyone else that there is more to them than what meets the eye."

Jane went completely still as the woman's

words seemed to penetrate some kind of invisible shield she'd maintained over the innermost workings of her mind...of her heart.

Bette looked into the camera and Jane felt as if the woman were speaking directly to her. "Remember, it is easier to live with rejection than to live with regret. You owe it to yourself to be the authentic you."

"But some women are happy being demure," Eve pointed out.

"I'm not talking about the women who are truly happy with their quiet existence," Bette said. "I'm talking about the woman who is sad...lonely... restless."

Jane swallowed hard—she was all of those things. This edgy feeling that had been festering inside her since that loser James had dumped her...was it her inner self trying to tell her that she deserved better? That the reason she hadn't met her soul mate was because she was presenting a false front to the world?

"Okay," Eve said, "let's say some of our viewers are out there thinking 'yes, that's me.' What can she do to let out that inner wild child?

"The process is different for every woman— sometimes it's as simple as giving yourself permission to let that wild child out of the closet. Sometimes it takes more drastic action, such as a makeover, or a change of scenery."

A change of scenery…that's what she needed. A place where she could experiment with this wild child theory in private…away from the prying eyes of people who would judge her. A weekend jaunt far away from Atlanta.

Her heart fluttered with excitement, but as her mind fast-forwarded through the details, she realized that her finances were already likely to be strained from repairing the dent in her car…and possibly buying a new tire. Her mouth tightened in renewed anger toward Perry Brewer, then she sighed in resignation.

Financial reality came first.

Jane turned down the volume on the set monitor, reached for the phone and the yellow pages, and reluctantly put plans for unleashing her inner wild child on hold until she had some spare cash. Maybe next month. Or next year…

5

"So, HOW'D IT GO?" Theresa asked him on the phone.

"I feel good about my closing," Perry cautiously told his long-time office manager. "But the judge postponed his decision until next week."

"Perry, I don't think we can hang on that long. Your creditors are breathing down my neck."

"What about the money from the sale of my house?"

"We've already gone through it."

He pinched the bridge of his nose to ward off the headache that threatened. "Put them off for a few more days, Theresa. When the judge rules in our favor and orders Deartmond Industries to pay, we'll be back on top."

"Don't you mean *if* the judge rules in your favor and orders Deartmond Industries to pay? I think it's great that you took on this case pro bono, but you've spent so much time on it, your revenues have hit bottom. If you lose this case, or if the compensation isn't spectacular, we'll have to close the doors." She made a rueful noise. "Perhaps you should consider taking the settlement."

He set his jaw. "The settlement is an insult to my client. And besides, it's no longer on the table."

"This newfound nobility of yours is admirable, Perry, but it was easier to pay the bills when you were an ambulance chaser."

He laughed at her dry humor. "Have some faith. I'll find some way to pay the bills."

She sighed. "When are you coming in? You have about a hundred phone calls to return."

"I'll be there after lunch. I need to stop by my condo first."

"So, how is condo living?"

He frowned into the phone. "Apparently, the walls are thin. I miss my house."

"Win that judgment and you can move," Theresa said flatly.

Perry pursed his mouth. "Which reminds me—

would you run down a bio on a woman named Jane Kurtz? She lives in my building, so she'll have the same address."

"Is this someone you're trying to hit on?" she asked suspiciously.

"No," he said with a frown. Although strangely, the idea wasn't completely unappealing.

"Okay, well, I have to go so I can make a deal with the devil to keep our lights on for another week."

"You're the best," Perry said.

"Yes, I am," Theresa agreed, then hung up.

He switched off the hands-free microphone and exhaled while loosening his tie. The Kendall case had already drawn out eighteen months longer than he'd expected, and had consumed an enormous amount of time. He'd passed on other cases and was now operating his law firm on a shoestring, but he'd thought it was worth it when he'd taken on security guard Thomas Kendall's case. His employer, Deartmond Industries, had exposed Kendall to dangerous emissions over two decades as he manned his post in a guard shack situated next to the manufacturer's exhaust system, then fired him when the man had applied for disability over the lung ailment he had developed.

In hindsight, Perry still believed in the case. He only hoped he didn't wind up filing for bankruptcy for his principles. The Kendall case was all or nothing—if they won, and if the reparations were as big as Perry thought they should be, Thomas Kendall could afford a lung transplant and he and his family would be set for the rest of their lives. And Perry's law firm would recover. But if they lost, or if the reparations were less than the trivial amount the company had offered as a settlement, then Perry was sunk and his client would suffer, too.

Maybe Theresa was right—maybe he should go back to ambulance-chasing instead of trying to take on the world. After all, no good deed went unpunished.

As he approached his condo building, his mind turned away from his immediate problems to his *more* immediate problem—Jane Kurtz. He wasn't sure why the woman had gotten under his skin.

After all, he'd apologized for the harsh things he'd said about her.

Perry frowned. But instead of being angry or indignant, she'd acted as if she...deserved it. *I have a mirror. I know that I'm not...exciting.* And she hadn't been fishing for compliments—she'd been very matter-of-fact.

Apparently the woman had grown up thinking—or being told—that she wasn't as pretty as other girls. He didn't like the idea that he was one of the people who had added to the woman's impression of herself. It shouldn't be a big thing... but somehow it was.

When he pulled into the parking garage and rounded the corner to the guest parking area, he glanced over to see if she'd gotten her flat fixed and did a double-take when he noticed her sprawling on her stomach next to the tire, inserting a jack under the frame, a spare tire lying nearby. He wheeled his vehicle into the closest spot and climbed out. She turned her head as he strode toward her.

"Thought you were going to call a repair service," he said.

She looked back to her task. "I did, but they were going to charge a fortune, and it wasn't in my budget this month. I did this a couple of times in college. It's not that hard."

Perry was listening—sort of. He was distracted by the sight of her shapely behind that was outlined as she strained to get the jack in place. Wow, plain little Jane Kurtz was hiding some curves under those boyish clothes.

He rolled up his sleeves and lowered himself to the ground next to her. "Let me give you a hand."

"I can do it," she said, sounding irritated.

She probably didn't realize that she had a streak of grease across her nose. "I'm sure you can," he said easily. "But I can do it more quickly. And besides, it would make me feel better about this whole parking situation."

She hesitated.

"Please," he added.

She finally gave a curt nod and scooted out to allow him access to the jack.

He situated the jack, then retreated to reach for the wrench she had lain nearby.

"I already loosened the lug nuts," she offered.

He nodded—so she did know what she was doing. He used his foot to operate the jack, slowly at first to make sure it was stable, then continued raising the car until the flat tire was about six inches off the ground. He used the wrench to remove the lug nuts and set them aside. After he pulled off the tire, he examined the nail sticking out of it. "I'll buy you a new tire."

She stood nearby, arms crossed, watching him. "That's not necessary."

"I think it is."

"Look, Mr. Brewer—"

"Call me Perry."

"P-Perry…don't feel like you owe me something because…" She blushed furiously, then raised her chin. "Because of what you said."

He stood to set the ruined tire aside. "I don't. I feel like I owe you because my guest took your parking place. If she had parked here, I'd be doing this for her."

"Oh." She averted her gaze.

He placed the spare tire on the wheel, replaced

the lug nuts, and lowered the car to the ground before giving the nuts a final twist. He returned the jack and lug wrench to their storage space in the trunk and closed it, then pulled a handkerchief from his pocket to wipe his hands.

Jane stood there watching, hugging herself. "Thank you."

He walked over to stand in front of her, noticing how her crossed arms accentuated her breasts, which were damn impressive considering how slender she was. He dragged his gaze upward, then lifted the corner of his handkerchief to her face.

She stiffened.

"You have a smudge," he murmured, then wiped off the dark grease slashing across her nose.

A nice nose, he conceded, pert and well-shaped... above a nice pink mouth that had parted slightly, and below a pair of cornflower blue eyes that were nice, now that they weren't swollen and red.

A hank of light brown hair had escaped from her ponytail and fell across her eyebrow like a shiny satin ribbon. He reached up to finger it aside, and the baby fine silkiness sent a jolt through him.

Jane pulled back, a slight frown marring her forehead. "Are we finished here?"

He dropped his hand and stuffed the handkerchief back in his pocket. "Yes. I'll replace your tire as soon as possible, today if I can arrange it."

"Thank you."

"No problem," he said, then picked up the damaged tire and headed toward his SUV.

"Perry," she called out from behind him.

He turned.

"How did you do? On your case, I mean."

An involuntary smile curved his mouth—of all the women in his life, only Theresa ever asked about his cases, and that was strictly business. "I won't know until next week, but I have a good feeling about this one."

A shy smile lifted her mouth.

"But if you'd keep your fingers crossed for me," he said with a grin, "I'd appreciate it."

JANE'S BREATH caught at the sight of Perry's grin that was intended just for her. To say that the man had surprised her would be an understatement.

He'd been…*nice*. And he looked…*sexy*. Feeling as if she'd just been sprinkled with stardust, she stood rooted to the spot as he climbed into the SUV, waved, and drove off in the opposite direction.

Then she banged her palm against her forehead. *Idiot*. It was all part of his schtick…his game…his strategy to get back in her good graces. She frowned and jammed her hands on her hips. Perry Brewer was the kind of man who wanted women to adore him…and she was sure there were plenty who did. But she wasn't going to fall for Nasty Boy's oozing charm.

Resolving to be immune to his smoke-and-mirrors magnetism, she climbed into her car and drove back to the office, stopping at a drive-through to pick up a sandwich. Her thoughts wandered to Liza because they often went out for lunch together, or picked up carry-out to take back to the office and have lunch with Eve. Now Liza was gone and Eve was far too busy to stop and enjoy an unhurried meal.

Facing an afternoon of staff meetings, Jane parked her car and reexamined the dent in her door.

She'd have to weigh the cost of having it fixed herself versus turning it in on her insurance and paying the deductible. She sighed and headed into the station, again wondering what the show's progress would mean for her...for all of them. More money, hopefully, although Eve was clearly the talent and the windfall would rightfully fall her way.

Jane smirked. She'd settle for enough extra cash to take that long, daring weekend to another horizon that she'd dreamed about during this morning's show. Bette Valentine had certainly hit a nerve. Too bad Jane wasn't in a position to do anything about it. She went into the makeup room and turned up the monitor that played the cable's fledgling noon news program, then unwrapped her soggy club sandwich.

"And here are the Lot O' Bucks lottery numbers that were released just moments ago. Officials report one winning ticket for the thirty-eight-million-dollar prize, so pay attention." The anchor read off the six numbers and Jane repeated the familiar numbers in her head as she chewed.

Then she realized the six numbers were familiar

because they were the six numbers she and four coworkers played twice a quarter. Her particular number, one of the two original numbers she had pooled with Eve and Liza, was "1."

The loneliest number.

The most unimaginative.

But today, the first of six winning numbers.

Jane swallowed and pushed to her feet slowly, her lunch forgotten. She reached for her purse and frantically fished through her wallet for the lottery ticket that she'd purchased for them. With her heart galloping in her chest, she confirmed the date and the numbers one by one to the numbers scrolling across the television screen.

The hand holding the ticket began to shake.

They'd won.

She was…a millionaire.

6

FEELING FAINT, Jane walked, then jogged to Eve's office, where Eve and her personal assistant were poring over stacks of paper and eating take-out.

Jane rapped on the glass door. Eve looked up, then smiled and gestured for her to come in.

"Sorry to interrupt," Jane said, stepping inside.

"No, it's fine," Eve said, reaching to snag a French fry from a box. "What's up?"

Jane glanced at Eve's personal assistant. "Uh… I need to talk to Eve alone, please."

Eve frowned, then asked for her assistant to give them some privacy.

As soon as the door closed, Eve sat forward. "Is something wrong?"

"No," Jane said, suddenly nervous all over again. She uncurled her hand to reveal the lottery ticket.

Eve reached for her purse. "Is it time to pitch in again for a ticket?"

"Eve…we won."

Her friend was still rummaging in her purse, half listening. "Hmm?"

"We. Won."

Eve's head snapped up. "What do you mean we won? We won…the lottery?"

Jane nodded solemnly, feeling like she was about to come out of her skin.

Then Eve laughed. "What did we match—two numbers? Enough for a free play?"

Jane wet her lips. "Eve, we got all six numbers. We *won*."

She finally had Eve's attention. Her friend's eyes widened. "Is this a joke?"

"No."

Eve grabbed the ticket and turned to her computer to log on to the lottery's Web site. With hurried movements, she clicked until she found the day's winning numbers, then cross-checked them against the ticket. "Omigod," she murmured. "What's the payout?"

Jane hesitated, almost afraid to utter the words. "Thirty…eight…million."

Eve gasped and covered her mouth. "But there must be other winning tickets, it can't be that much."

"The announcer said there was only one winning ticket."

Eve stood. "But that means…" Her mouth fell open, then her face erupted in a stunned grin. "Jane…we're rich!"

They fell into each other's arms, squealing and jumping up and down. Jane felt as if she were going to fly apart.

"We have to let Nicole know!" Eve exclaimed. "And Zach, and Cole!"

Jane nodded excitedly. Nicole Reavis was their segment-story producer who had taken Liza's position and had asked to get in on the collective lottery ticket. Zach Haas, a favorite cameraman, had also asked to join them, and Cole Crawford, the show's supervising producer, the man who had "discovered" Eve, was their fifth cohort.

All of their lives would be forever changed, she

realized as Eve grabbed her phone and began dialing. Jane's thoughts jumped to Liza—playing the lottery had been something the three of them had done for fun. And now that the unthinkable had happened, Liza was missing out...

"HERE'S THE INFORMATION you wanted on your neighbor, Jane Kurtz," Theresa said, handing Perry a sheet of paper. "She's pretty, but she doesn't look like your type."

"She isn't," Perry agreed, studying a copy of the picture from her driver's license. She looked awkward and camera-shy. Then he frowned and looked up. "What's my type?"

Theresa shrugged. "You know—flashy...interchangeable."

Her response rankled, although he conceded that there was a sameness about Kayla and Cindi and Kendra and Victoria. And Denise and Cassandra and Fiona. "Hey, Ms. Kurtz works on that show you like, *Just Between Us*," he said.

"Really? Yeah, today's show was great—unleashing your inner wild child." She batted her eyelashes and touched a hand to her graying hair. "Think I'm too old for that?"

"Never."

She laughed, then squinted. "How did you get grease on your shirt?"

"I had to buy Ms. Kurtz a new tire," he said, scanning the paper.

"Oh. The plot thickens. Is Ms. Kurtz needy?"

"No, but she's on a budget, and since I indirectly caused her to have a flat tire and a dent in her car, I figured it was the least I could do." He walked toward his office, ignoring the sting of Theresa's curiosity burning a hole in his back. He dropped into his chair and surveyed the profile on his prim little neighbor.

Jane Kurtz, age thirty-one, birthplace Columbus, Georgia, an only child, born to William and Maria Kurtz, both deceased. He glanced at their birthdates and realized they had been older when Jane was born. She was probably raised in a sheltered environment…and now she was alone.

Perry bit down on his tongue. He couldn't imagine that feeling—his parents were alive and healthy, he had two brothers and two sisters, plus a herd of nieces and nephews. Jane Kurtz would be swallowed whole by his family.

Not that she would ever meet his family, he reminded himself.

There was no college degree listed, so either she hadn't attended or hadn't finished. Employed with Cable One Communications for three years, registered owner of a beige 1997 Honda Civic, no police record, no traffic violations, not even a parking ticket.

His mouth curled into a smirk—her lawfulness didn't surprise him. Jane Kurtz was the kind of woman who would never think of removing the "Do Not Remove" tag from a mattress, who probably always washed her hair twice because the shampoo bottle said so.

His thoughts skipped to the silkiness of her hair as he'd swept it back from her face. What would it feel like to sink both hands into the depths of that honey-colored hair? Would those cornflower blue eyes turn dark if she were aroused? And had that pink mouth of hers ever been thoroughly kissed?

Chastising himself for letting his imagination run away with him, he set aside the paper and thoughts of plain Jane Kurtz, turning his attention to returning phone calls and processing paperwork of neglected cases. He and Theresa both worked late to catch up on things he'd allowed to slide while he'd labored over the Kendall case. Around six o'clock, he had Chinese food delivered.

While they were eating, Theresa pointed a chopstick at him. "You need a vacation."

"I know," he muttered. "I'll take one…someday."

"Why don't you take some time this weekend?" she asked. "You're not going to hear anything about the Kendall case until next week. You need to recharge, Perry, so you can get this firm back on its feet."

He gave a dry laugh. "I can't afford to take a vacation."

"You have a million frequent flyer miles—use them."

"I'll think about it," he promised.

"Hey, look," she said, pointing to the TV set in the corner of the room. "Someone won the lottery."

The volume was down, but the picture showed a group of people crowded around a podium. Theresa reached for the remote and turned up the sound.

"Five coworkers of Cable One Communications who work on the popular *Just Between Us* talk show have come forward with today's winning Lot O' Bucks ticket to claim just over thirty-eight million dollars."

"We were just talking about that show," Theresa said.

The camera panned the winners quickly, and anyone not looking for the slight woman with the honey-colored ponytail would've missed her.

"That's her," Perry said, lurching forward. "That's Jane Kurtz!"

Theresa gave a little laugh and went back to her fried rice. "Looks like you didn't have to spring for that tire after all. Something tells me that Jane Kurtz will be buying a whole new car."

7

"ARE YOU STILL walking on air?" Eve asked.

Jane laughed into her phone. "When I left this morning, my life was normal, and now I'm driving home a millionaire—it's mind-boggling."

"I still can't believe it," Eve said. "Everyone is calling for an interview. This is a media storm! Are you sure you don't want to participate?"

"I'm sure," Jane said. "I'm not comfortable in front of the camera. You guys can handle it. Have you decided what to do about the show?"

"No…but a couple of days of hiatus will do everyone some good, I think."

Jane smirked—Cole Crawford was no dummy. Putting the show on hiatus would free up Eve to appear on *other* talk shows and raise her visibility. With the money at their disposal, he and Eve could form their own production company…the sky was the limit. "It'll be nice to have a couple of days to let things soak in," she agreed.

"What are you going to do first?" Eve asked. "Something sensible, I'm sure. Maybe buy a new car, but nothing too fancy?"

She knew her friend was only teasing, but the realization that people expected her to do something…*expected* rankled her. "I don't know. I might surprise everyone."

"Right," Eve said dryly. "And do what? Buy a new TV? A new washer and dryer?"

"Maybe," Jane conceded, then squirmed in her seat. "I haven't wrapped my mind around the possibilities yet."

"Oh, that's Cole beeping in. Can I talk to you later?"

"Sure," Jane said. "Talk soon."

"Okay."

Jane disconnected the call and gripped the steering wheel tight. The day had been surreal— the trip to the lottery office, signing the back of the ticket, attending the hastily-arranged press conference. She had hung back, allowing her more camera-ready friends to answer questions from the media. Her mind still reeled with the wonder of having so much money. Her parents, God rest their souls, would never have been able to grasp the concept of her share.

"Six point three million dollars," she murmured, testing the number on her tongue. Then she grinned. "Six point three million dollars," she said, louder. "Six point three million dollars!" she shouted, pounding on the steering wheel.

The man sitting in the car next to her in traffic looked at her as if she was crazy, sending a flush to climb her face. She settled back in her seat, but a smile crept over her mouth. "Six point three million dollars," she whispered.

She wondered if anyone else knew—and who she should tell. Most of her friends were her co-workers, so they knew. As far as her neighbors…

Perry Brewer. A smirk curved her mouth. She wouldn't have to put up with his noisy shenanigans much longer. She could afford to buy a nicer condo…or a big house where she wouldn't have to share a wall with anyone.

She could, she realized, have almost anything she wanted.

Dinner, for instance. She could go to that expensive restaurant in Buckhead that she'd been hearing about. But she didn't want to go out alone. On impulse, she called the restaurant and asked if they delivered. They did, the woman informed her, but there was a hefty delivery charge.

Jane bit into her lip. "How much?"

"Thirty-five dollars," was the crisp response.

Jane winced, then realized that she was going to have to start thinking like a rich woman. "That's fine. I'll have a lobster tail, a Caesar salad, and a bottle of your best chardonnay."

"I'll need a credit card number, ma'am."

Jane swallowed and realized that until her share of the winnings was wired into her bank account, she'd have to float expenses on her American Express card. She gave the charge information to the woman, but nearly changed her mind when presented with the total of more than two hundred dollars. She reminded herself that she could afford it…that it was a first-in-a-lifetime splurge to celebrate a turning point in her life.

She pulled into the condo parking lot and wheeled into her assigned spot, noticing that Perry's vehicle wasn't there. Maybe she would get a reprieve this evening from the explicit antics next door. Unbidden, snatches of the couple's lovemaking sounds came back to her, sending a tingle to her midsection and warmth to her cheeks. She did not want to have to listen to that again…absolutely not…

When she unlocked the door to the condo, she walked in and flipped on lights, feeling antsy. She set down her bag and paced the length of her condo. Then she shed her work clothes and took a long, hot shower, for once not caring about her water bill, and telling herself she would buy French milled soap as soon as she figured out where to buy it.

And one of those nice, waffle spa robes, she thought as she shrugged into her pink terrycloth standby. And nice towels, she decided as she wrapped her hair turban-style in one of her discount finds. Her phone rang, indicating her food delivery. She buzzed the man into the building and met him at her front door, signing for the largest tip she'd ever given anyone. But the aromas wafting from the foiled box were decadent, and the wine was chilled to perfection.

This was how the other half lived.

She spread the feast on her dining room table, thinking only last night she'd been eating Chinese food on her couch, with no idea how her life was about to change.

What a difference a day made.

She put on a Tristan Prettyman CD, in the mood for the folksy love songs, and trying to be proactive about filling her space with noise to help insulate her from any sound coming through the walls. She had just started the Caesar salad and was a glass into the bottle of wine when her doorbell rang. Jane frowned, not expecting anyone. She carried her glass of wine to the door and checked the peep hole. Her stomach did a little flip, then she swung open the door to the smiling face she'd once found very attractive.

"Hello, James."

"Jane...sweetheart." He leaned forward and hugged her, not noticing her lack of participation. "I hope you don't mind me dropping by like this."

"What do you want, James?"

He looked contrite. "I want you to forgive me for being so stupid."

Jane pressed her lips together. "Can you be more specific?"

"I miss you."

"Really?"

"Yes. I've been meaning to call you for weeks, but I didn't think you'd talk to me. Then I saw you on TV, heard about the big news." He held up a bottle of wine. "I thought I'd help you celebrate. I knew you'd be alone."

She was trying to decide if that was an insult when footsteps sounded in the hallway. Jane looked up to see Perry Brewer walking toward them. His gaze focused on her and James, and she suddenly realized that she was in her robe, obviously fresh from the shower.

"Hello, Jane," Perry said.

"Hi, Perry."

The men looked at each other.

"James, this is my neighbor, Perry Brewer. Perry, this is James Watling, uh, a friend of mine."

"I'm her ex," James offered with his handshake.

"I see," Perry said, then turned back to Jane. "I have your tire in my SUV. I'd be glad to change it if you'll give me the key to your trunk."

James looked back and forth between them. Jane felt a little burst of retribution that he obviously thought something was going on between her and Perry. "Let me get them," she said cheerfully.

When she walked inside, James followed and set the bottle of wine on her counter. She fished her keys out of her purse, then backtracked to the door and handed them to Perry. "Thanks."

"No problem," Perry said, then hesitated, as if he wanted to say something else. Instead he glanced behind her at James, then back to her. "I'm going to change clothes, so it'll take me a few minutes."

"Just ring the doorbell," she said, then took a sip from her glass.

He nodded and turned toward his own door.

Jane closed her door, then frowned at James. "You interrupted my dinner."

"Is there enough for two? It smells great."

"Sorry," she said, not sorry at all.

"How about a glass of wine then? For old times' sake."

Jane chewed on her lip, studying the man. She remembered his parting words to her, that she was a bore. Apparently her newfound fortune made her more interesting. "I don't think so, James."

He walked up to her and rubbed her upper arms. "Jane, we had a good thing…we just let it get stale. Come on. One glass of wine. I just want to talk, catch up."

"One glass," she agreed, reluctantly admitting that having company tonight—even James—was better than being alone.

He grinned and helped himself to a glass from her cabinet. After he poured the wine, he lifted his glass. "To your new life. I hope there's a place in it for me." His eyes glittered with hope and…affection?

She allowed him to clink his glass against hers. Then she took a fortifying gulp of the wine.

8

PERRY SLAMMED Jane's car trunk with more force than necessary, then jammed his hands on his hips. Jane wins the lottery and her ex-boyfriend shows up at her door? Surely she could see through that, couldn't she?

The guy was smarmy. Perry could tell by his body language, his weak handshake…and the proprietary way he leaned toward Jane.

How long had they dated, he wondered? And how long ago had they split up? Had she been in love with this guy? Did she let him drive his hands into her silky hair?

Probably, Perry reasoned as he backtracked to her condo door and rang the doorbell. Because the guy probably hadn't called her a homely little geek. The guy probably made her feel…pretty.

She swung open the door.

And she was pretty, Perry realized with a start. Her cheeks were pink and her eyes bright, her mouth plump and shiny. Slender legs extended from the knee-length robe she wore, and at the thought that she was probably nude beneath, his cock jumped in his jeans.

"Did you finish?" she asked.

"Uh, yes," he said, then pulled her keys from his pocket.

She took the keys and he noticed that her hands were graceful, her fingers long, her nails natural and of a practical length. "That was very nice of you," she said. "Thank you."

"You're welcome," he murmured, bewildered over his sudden physical awareness of this woman. It was the wine, he thought. It gave her a languid look. It was the way she might look in the throes of lovemaking.

"Good night," she said, and started to close the door.

"Uh, Jane."

She opened the door. "Yes?"

"I, um, saw you on the news. Wow—congratulations."

She smiled. "Thanks. It was rather unexpected...I don't think it's sunk in yet."

He glanced past her and saw James standing next to her balcony door in the distance. "Jane, I don't mean to pry, but have you contacted an attorney?"

"No. Why should I?"

"Because once people find out that you won the lottery, they'll be coming out of the woodwork trying to get next to you."

"Is that so?"

"Yes."

She took another sip of wine. "I appreciate your concern, but I think I can handle it."

Then she closed the door in his face.

Perry straightened, then grimaced. Obviously, she couldn't wait to get back to her ex. Was the guy trying to wheedle his way into her life again, with his eye on her multi-million-dollar bank account?

He returned to his own condo and pulled a beer out of the fridge, irritated at everything in general and nothing in particular. He switched on the TV and watched a few minutes of a football game, but found his mind wandering. He glanced at the wall he and Jane shared. Was it his imagination, or had her music gotten louder? Perry scowled and stood, then walked to the wall and pressed his ear against it.

Nothing. But maybe they didn't make noise when they made out. Maybe Jane was the quiet type who bit her lover's shoulder when she came.

Then Perry smirked. *If* the guy could make her come. He took another pull off the beer and walked out onto his balcony, his pulse quickening when he heard their voices on the other side of the wall.

"We had a lot of good things going, Jane. Let's give it another try."

Perry rolled his eyes, then strained to hear her response, but it was too low. The sound of her balcony door sliding closed let him know they had gone back inside.

To seal the deal?

Perry realized with a startling clarity that he was jealous. Jealous that someone else would get close to Jane before he could show her that he hadn't meant what he said…that they could be friends…

And more?

With that disturbing thought rattling around in his head, he retreated to the living room and forced himself to stare at the television. But subconsciously he was keeping his ears perked for any sounds of physical contact next door. The thought of that guy cajoling her into bed made his skin crawl. Jane deserved better than that.

He woke up in the wee hours of the morning sprawled on the couch, his television a static "Off Air" picture. Perry dragged himself up and stumbled to bed, wondering if Jane's guest had slept over. All was quiet next door as far as he could tell. Was she curled up next to her ex, her hair spilled on the pillow?

He fell into a fitful sleep, and when his alarm sounded, he still felt groggy. A shower revived him, but he couldn't shake the disgruntled feeling from the previous night.

He was pouring a cup of coffee when he thought he heard Jane's door opening and closing. He yanked up the mug, grabbed his briefcase, and headed to his door, driven by the unexplainable need to know if what's-his-name had spent the night, had wormed his way back into Jane's life in time to squander her money.

He walked into the hallway and relief bled through him to see only Jane standing there locking her door. "Good morning," he said.

"Good morning," she returned.

She was wearing snug jeans and a blue ringer T-shirt, plus sneakers, and her ever-present pony-tail. He glanced over her figure with appreciation, then he noticed her suitcase and frowned. "Going somewhere?"

She straightened and looked up at him. "If you must know, then yes. And actually, I have you to thank."

"Me?"

"Yes." She smiled. "You're the one who made me realize just how boring my life is. But now I have the money to change that."

He couldn't very well protest. "Where are you going?" To visit an old aunt, he hoped.

She grinned. "I'm flying to Vegas."

He frowned. "Vegas?"

"That's right."

"With that guy James?"

"No." She lifted her chin. "All by myself. To see if the city lives up to the commercials. To have a blowout weekend of pure, unadulterated fun." She picked up her suitcase.

"That's not a very big suitcase."

"I don't plan to be wearing much," she said cheerfully. "See you later, neighbor."

Perry stood stock still, watching her walk away, her ponytail and rear end swinging. *Damn.*

"W-wait," he called, locking his door and hurrying to catch up with her on the stairs. "Are you planning to gamble?"

"Yes," she answered, trotting down the stairs happily.

"But do you think that's a good idea? I mean, do you know how to gamble?"

"Nope," she said as they reached the parking garage. "But I'm going to try everything."

"Vegas can be a dangerous place," he warned.

She opened her car door and tossed her suitcase inside. "I hope so! Bye."

Perry stood helplessly and watched her drive away. Because of the stupid things he'd said, she was going to Vegas to do God knows what, unaware that there were hordes of professional con men out there who would see her coming a mile away. Any man who had sisters was sensitive to the trouble naive young women could unwittingly find themselves in, especially if they were looking for a little attention.

After all, Perry thought with a frown, men were basically jerks who were driven by the need to satisfy their own selfish desires.

It takes one to know one, Brewer.

Rankled, he climbed into his SUV and loosened his tie, his mind swirling with possible scenarios. Someone could slip a mickey in her drink. Rob her. Assault her. Or charm her into bed. Spend her money. She could come home broke…injured. Or with a disease…

All because of what he'd said.

Perry set his jaw, then opened his cell phone and called his office. Theresa answered on the first ring.

"You're late."

"I've decided to take that vacation after all," he said. "I'll be back in the office Monday morning."

"Mind if I ask where you're going?"

"I'm going to Vegas."

9

JANE HAD NEVER flown first class before—it was like traveling in a private coach, with flight attendants at your beck and call, and more food and drink than she could possibly consume. But even the in-flight movie couldn't keep her mind off the words she'd spoken with such bravado to Perry Brewer. She wouldn't be wearing very many clothes? She wanted to try everything in Vegas? She hoped it was dangerous? The words had spilled out of her mouth as if she were a different person.

Was it, she wondered, the voice of her inner wild child that Bette Valentine had told her was dying to get out?

Over a glass of pinot noir and a dish of warm nuts, she thought of James and shook her head. He had arrived on her doorstep with a lame apology for his behavior and thought he could convince her to pick up where they'd left off. She'd allowed him to drink a glass of wine and make a play for her affections. But when he'd suggested that they give their relationship another try, she'd told him unequivocally, irrevocably, absolutely *no.* James had been shocked, then angry. And then he'd recovered his composure and told her that she could call him when she got lonely.

It was then that she'd decided that she wasn't going to get lonely—that she was going somewhere far away from Atlanta for that wild, anonymous weekend she'd dreamed of.

But as the wheels of the plane touched down, her heart hammered against her chest at the thought of living up to her rash words.

Was she really prepared to hook up with a complete stranger?

Her cell phone rang while she waited for a taxi. She glanced at the screen and smiled—it was Eve—then connected the call.

"Hi."

"Where are you?" Eve asked. "I've called a dozen times."

Jane wet her lips. "I'm in Vegas."

"Vegas?" Eve sounded incredulous. "*Las* Vegas? You're joking."

"No. I decided to come here for the weekend."

"Wow, I never thought—I mean, that's great, Jane. You *should* do something…"

"Wild?"

"I was going to say fun. Are you with James?"

"No. I'm alone." She couldn't decide if that sounded brave, or pathetic.

"Wow."

"Is everything okay there?"

"Uh…yeah. I was just wondering if maybe you'd heard from Liza."

"Liza? No. Have you?"

"No…not exactly."

"What exactly?"

"I've had a couple of hang-ups from a private number on my home phone."

"The lottery commission said we'd be getting

lots of calls. Maybe you should go ahead and change your number."

"But these calls had music playing in the background—the Ramones."

Liza's favorite group. "It's probably just a coincidence. If it were Liza, why wouldn't she have said something?"

"I don't know. Maybe she's in trouble."

Jane sighed. "We can't help her, Eve, if we don't even know where she is. Liza's a big girl. And she's the one who walked away from...everything." From her friends.

"You're right, of course," Eve said. "You're always the voice of reason, Jane." Then Eve laughed. "Which is why I can't believe you're in Vegas! What are you going to do out there by yourself?"

"I don't know," Jane said cheerfully. "Spend a lot of money, I guess."

"Hmm," Eve said, sounding perplexed. "Where are you staying?"

"At the Bellagio."

"Wow. When are you coming back?"

"Sunday night," Jane said, suddenly eager to end the call. "Here's my taxi, gotta run."

"Okay. Well…be careful."

Jane said goodbye and disconnected the call, wondering if her friend's reaction was out of concern, or the fact that Jane had done something so out of character?

She climbed into the taxi with her overnight bag and tamped down a spike of apprehension. Maybe she *was* getting in over her head.

Her nervousness mounted during the taxi ride to her hotel, as she got a close-up view of the soaring casinos and clubs, their neon signs and lights impressive even in broad daylight—she couldn't imagine how frantic the atmosphere would be at night.

As for the Bellagio hotel itself, the fountains alone took her breath away, with series of columns of water spraying into the sky, then falling like rows of dancers, only to rise again in another brilliant explosion.

Even the water in Vegas had pizzazz.

Walking into the hotel lobby, she felt like an awestruck schoolgirl. The centerpiece was an incredible Dale Chihuly glass sculpture, a riotous explosion of fused and intertwined flowers and vines so delicate in appearance that they defied the material they were made from. The piece was spellbinding, more beautiful even than the Chihuly pieces she'd seen on display in the Atlanta Botanical Gardens. At the time she wondered that individuals could afford to own a Chihuly piece privately.

And now, Jane realized suddenly, *she* could. The notion was still mind-boggling.

In addition to the sculpture, the lobby featured a conservatory and garden, soaring ceilings and levels that seemed to extend forever. She felt small and out of place in her casual clothes, holding her tiny overnight bag. Everyone around her looked like money—women wore designer dresses and high heels, men wore sport coats and western boots or expensive dress shoes. Self-consciously, she stepped up to the front desk to check in, but the pretty darkhaired desk clerk smiled warmly, putting her at ease.

"Welcome to Las Vegas," the woman said. "Are you here on vacation?"

Jane nodded. "The reservation is under Kurtz."

"Are you traveling alone, Ms. Kurtz?"

Jane nodded again.

The woman winked. "Probably not for long."

Jane blushed. She hoped the woman was right.

Looking up from her computer screen, the clerk said, "I'm sorry, Ms. Kurtz, but your suite isn't ready yet. How about a complimentary drink in one of our lounges?"

"Actually, I need to do some shopping and… maybe have my hair done."

The woman smiled wide. "The hotel salon is renowned, and they can usually handle walk-ins. And you're in luck—we have some of the best shopping in the city right here in the hotel." She handed Jane a brochure and indeed, every major designer seemed to have a presence. The knowledge that she could buy for herself all the clothes and accessories she'd coveted when she'd bought them for the talk show's wardrobe was still more than she could get her mind around.

"Thank you," Jane said in relief, grateful for the guidance. She felt out of her element here, where everything seemed bigger, brighter, and louder.

was pumping, too, at the thought of seeing Jane again, although he hadn't yet thought of a good explanation as to why he had followed her.

"The Bellagio," he said the cab driver, then climbed in, hoping to think of something plausible along the way.

Fancy meeting you here—didn't I mention I was also coming to Vegas?

I was worried that you would fall prey to some con artist, so I came to look out for you...

I couldn't stand the thought of you coming to Vegas to hook up with some stranger...

Perry pursed his mouth—the truth sounded so...proprietary. What if Jane wasn't happy to see him? What if she didn't want him to watch out for her?

But he kept telling himself that it was his careless words that had sent her running in search of fun, frivolity, and flirtation. If she wound up getting hurt, it would be his fault.

He walked into the Bellagio and scanned the expansive lobby, hoping for a glimpse of Jane's ponytail among the throng of people moving in and out. A pang of panic struck his stomach—what if he couldn't find her? She was so slight and so...passive, she could easily be lost in a crowd this size, swept away...misplaced.

Knowing his thoughts were running amok, he pulled his hand down his face to get a grip. Then he stepped up to the registration desk, his frown fading slightly at the warm smile of the brunette behind the desk. "Brewer, checking in," he said.

"Are you traveling alone, Mr. Brewer?"

"Actually...I'm meeting a friend here. Her name is Jane Kurtz. Can you tell me if she's checked in yet?"

"Yes, Ms. Kurtz checked in a few hours ago."

He leaned in and winked. "Actually, my being here is a surprise. I don't suppose you could give me her room number, could you?"

She surveyed his suit as if she was trying to deduce his believability.

"Please?" he added hopefully, unwilling to depend on the Pucci tie.

She tilted her head, then checked her computer

screen. "Well, technically, I can't tell you her room number, sir. But if you like, I can put you in a room very nearby."

He smiled wide. "Thank you. That would be terrific."

"You're welcome. I'm sure Ms. Kurtz will be happy to see you."

He kept smiling as he handed over his credit card, hoping she was right.

A bellman carried his hastily packed suitcase to his room. Perry tipped the man, then stepped back into the hall to glance at the doors around his. Two were nearby—one across the hall and one next door. As he stood there, the door across the hall opened abruptly, and a couple emerged, their arms draped around each other. That meant Jane must be in the other one. He nodded hello as the couple passed, then retreated to his room to freshen up and change into casual clothes. Then, rehearsing what he might say when Jane answered, he emerged from his room, walked to the remaining door and knocked.

Perry smoothed a hand over the back of his hair,

realizing with a start that he was nervous. When was the last time a woman had made him nervous?

Only because he was afraid she would think he was stalking her and slap him with a restraining order. But if she was angry, or didn't want to see him, he would honor her wishes and stay away from her.

It wasn't as if he was in love with her or anything.

He knocked again, thinking he might have missed her. Maybe she was already in the casino, playing recklessly and being hit on by every smarmy guy in the vicinity.

The door swung open and he took a step back to see a striking woman with white blond hair standing there, her manicured hand on a sleek shoulder bag, her hourglass figure highlighted in a black leather miniskirt and a low-cut fuchsia colored blouse. The bare, slender legs ended in sexy high-heeled black strappy sandals.

"I'm sorry, I'm looking for a friend of mine," he began.

"Perry?" the woman asked. "What are you doing here?"

His mind raced, wondering if he'd had the bad

luck of randomly running into an old flame, because the voice seemed oddly familiar. Then he noticed the large cornflower blue eyes, and he blinked in astonishment at the vision of the blonde vixen before him. *"Jane?"*

She crossed her arms, the movement accentuating breasts that threatened to spill out of her blouse. "In the flesh."

10

"IN THE FLESH" was right.

Perry's mind reeled as he tried to reconcile his memory of plain Jane Kurtz to the image of the sexpot standing before him. Her hair was pale, with layers framing her heart-shaped face. Her blue eyes were huge, highlighted with long, dark lashes and perfectly arched eyebrows. But her lush curves really threw him for a loop—he couldn't believe the woman had been hiding that killer bod beneath khakis and polo shirts. And those legs… God help him.

"Perry, what are you doing here?" she repeated.

"I…I, uh…" He was struck speechless, trying to remember what he'd rehearsed, but he was utterly confounded. "You look…amazing." That caught her off guard, he could tell by the way she softened.

"I do?"

He nodded and swallowed hard. "Yeah."

"Thank you," she said, then resumed her stance. "Did you follow me?"

As an attorney, he'd learned when not to lie. "Yes."

"Why?"

"Because I felt responsible for you going off on some wild weekend where you might get…"

"Laid?" she supplied dryly.

"Hurt," he corrected, irritated that she'd so squarely guessed his intentions. He gestured vaguely in the air. "There are all kinds of con artists out here just looking for someone like you to take advantage of."

"Someone like me?" She frowned. "Maybe I'm looking to be taken advantage of."

But the bravado of her words wasn't reflected in her eyes that, now highlighted with shadow and liner, were easier than ever to read. Perry gave her a little smile. "You don't mean that."

"I came out here to have fun," she insisted, gripping her purse in a way that made him wonder if she had rolls of quarters—or condoms—inside.

"I know," he conceded, then wet his lips. The most outrageous idea he'd ever had just popped into his head. "And I have a proposition for you."

She looked suspicious. "What do you mean?"

Perry broke out in a sweat along his hairline— this was new territory for him. "I was thinking… Instead of you hooking up with a complete stranger for the weekend, why not hook up with…me?"

JANE COULDN'T believe her ears. She stared at her decadently handsome neighbor as what he was suggesting began to sink in. "Hook up with *you?*"

Perry nodded and splayed his hands. "Why not? I'm a fun guy. I'll teach you how to gamble, take you wherever you want to go, do anything you want to…do."

Her cheeks warmed at his obvious implication.

"And," he continued, "you can feel safe."

Safe? She wanted to laugh. "Safe" wasn't the word for what she felt when she looked into Perry Brewer's bottomless dark eyes. The words "suspicious," "tense," and "petrified" came to mind.

Jane squinted up at him. "You're offering to *tutor* me in how to have a good time?"

He leaned on her doorframe and a wicked smile curved his mouth. "I guess I am."

A sensual shiver slid over her shoulders, but a sense of uneasiness plucked at her. Could Perry be after her new-won fortune? But the man was an attorney—he didn't need her money. The shoes he was wearing had easily cost six hundred dollars. "Wh-what's in this for you?"

"It'll make me feel better for my earlier, uh, ungentlemanly behavior."

Her eyebrows went up. "You mean for saying that I'm ugly?"

He straightened. "I didn't say that."

"No," she agreed. "I think your exact words were that I was a 'homely little geek who's probably never had a good lay.'"

He had the decency to cringe. "Not my finest hour. I'm sorry. I didn't mean it." Then he gestured to her outfit. "Any mirror will tell you how wrong I was about you being homely. Lady, you're gorgeous."

Her toes curled in her sandals. "No, I'm not."

He exhaled noisily, his eyes devouring her legs. "Yes, you are. And if you go downstairs to the casino alone, you'll have to beat the men off with a stick."

The notion was so ludicrous, she laughed.

Meanwhile, he seemed to sober. "Look, Jane, I was a jerk and I'd like a chance to make it up to you, that's all. Neither one of us is looking for a relationship. I need a vacation and you deserve to celebrate. Why don't we simply have fun together?"

Jane wavered, her mind spinning. His offer was so tempting—have fun with a sexy, charming man who wasn't a serial killer…that she knew of.

Even if Perry did do something…*objectionable,* she knew where the man lived. She frowned. That brought up another potential problem. "*If* I agreed to this proposition, as you put it, won't it be awkward when we get back to Atlanta?"

He shrugged. "I assume you won't be living in the building much longer, so I can't see it being an issue."

She pursed her mouth. That was true. She could buy a big house in Buckhead…or on the coast for that matter…any coast. One thing was certain. She no longer had to live in a condo with thin walls.

He extended his hand and grinned. "Come on, I'll buy you dinner. I'm starving. We'll talk about it and afterward, if you want me to take a hike, I will."

Jane looked at his hand. What was the harm? It was only dinner, and he was paying. He was right—he owed her that much for being a jerk.

She lifted her hand tentatively, then put it in his. As his warm fingers wrapped around hers, a jolt of awareness shot up her arm. Her gaze locked with his and she thought she saw reflected in his dark eyes the same sensations she was experiencing—surprise and trepidation. A split-second later she decided she'd been mistaken as his eyes filled with…desire? Her chest billowed with nervous excitement.

As they walked to the elevator, Jane felt stiff and self-conscious in the new clothes and shoes, but Perry put her at ease with small talk about what kind of food she liked to eat and pointing out attractions along the way. While they were being led to a table inside the restaurant he suggested, she noticed people looking their way and wondered if everyone thought they made an odd couple—after all, Perry was a strikingly handsome man.

Suddenly he clasped her hand in his again. "Jane, you'd better get used to people looking at you."

Her cheeks warmed with shock. People were looking at *her?* She passed a mirrored panel and indeed, it took her a moment to realize she was seeing herself. When the woman at the salon had turned her around to face the mirror, she'd barely been able to believe the transformation. And even though she saw the appreciation reflected in Perry's eyes, she was feeling a little like Cinderella...that if she made one wrong move, the spell would be broken and she'd go back to being plain Jane Kurtz.

The restaurant was finely furnished, with dark woods and pale upholstery. Each table was lavished with fresh flowers and immaculate table cloths. The diners were well-dressed and attentive to a jazz quartet playing on a slightly elevated stage before a small dance floor. Fantastic aromas wafted all around them.

When they reached their table, Perry released her hand and pulled out her chair. Jane hesitated, unable to remember when or if any man had ever held out a chair for her. She wasn't even sure what to do. Gingerly, she lowered herself into the chair and sat immobile while Perry slid the chair—and her—forward until she was comfortably tucked underneath the table.

The waiter nodded with approval as Perry took his own seat across from her, then he plucked her napkin from the table, opened it with a flourish, and handed it to her. She thanked him and smoothed the crisp linen cloth over her lap, wondering if being in Vegas had awakened her senses…or if she could attribute it to the man sitting across from her.

As if he could read her mind, Perry winked at her.

The waiter handed them menus, then asked for their drink order.

"Red wine?" Perry asked her.

She nodded. "You choose."

He ordered a bottle of Chilean wine in a varietal that she'd never heard of. She busied herself studying the menu, a little overwhelmed by the selection.

"It all looks good," he offered. "What are you in the mood for?"

At the sensual note in his voice, she looked up, a thrill barbing through her to find his attention on her. And she had a feeling that he wasn't referring solely to food.

"I'm not sure," she said honestly, then swallowed hard. "Anything."

"Anything?" he asked, one side of his mouth curving up. After a few seconds of pulsating silence, he cleared his throat. "How about if we experiment and order one of each of the tapas to share?"

She nodded, thinking there was something intimate about sharing food, but eager to try the appetizer-size dishes whose descriptions of exotic meats and unique combinations had her mouth watering.

Then she stole a glance at Perry, skimming the contours of his broad torso and admitted with a shiver that *he* might be responsible for her mouth watering.

The waiter returned with their bottle of wine and after pouring each of them a glass, took their order. When the young man left, Perry lifted his glass toward her. "A toast—to having fun."

She smiled and clinked her glass to his, then drank deeply of the inky wine, reveling in the smooth, rich flavors of fruit with the hint of something woodsy. "What is this called again?"

"Carmenere," he said. "Right now only the Chileans are bottling this grape varietal by itself. Do you like it?"

"Very much."

His smile lit his eyes as he lifted the bottle to top off her glass. "Good. Have you traveled much, Jane?"

She shook her head self-consciously. "I've always wanted to, though."

"So now you'll be able to."

She nodded, wondering if Eve would be able to get away for the two of them to travel together. Otherwise, while seeing the world would be a wonderful adventure, doing it alone would be slightly less fun.

His mouth turned downward in a sudden frown. "I don't want to belabor this point, but you really should consider getting a tax attorney and a financial planner to help you sort through this lottery business."

She took another drink from her glass, uncomfortable with mixing business and pleasure. "The people at the lottery office gave us the same advice. I will if I think it's necessary."

He pursed his mouth. "How well do you know the coworkers who won with you?"

She smiled. "Well enough to know that there won't be any trouble where they're concerned."

"This kind of money changes people," he warned.

She lifted her glass again for her own toast. "In my case, I certainly hope so."

Perry angled his head, but whatever he'd been about to say was lost when the waiter returned with the first round of tapas dishes they'd ordered. Plate after plate of sizzling, aromatic, and decorative foods were set on the table between them, and once again her pulse spiked at the intimacy of sharing food with Perry…a man she'd met only days ago but who seemed to have insinuated himself into her life out of guilt.

As she surveyed the slices of duck served over plantains, lump crab cakes with mango salsa, chorizo with figs, and almond-stuffed dates wrapped with prosciutto, her appetite suddenly kicked in with a vengeance. It was the sheer decadence and variety of the food that set her senses on tilt…along with the knowledge that from this point on, life was a feast. She felt giddy as she lifted bite-size portions onto her plate. When she forked a sliver of duck into her mouth, she moaned with pleasure, a noise that captured Perry's attention.

"You like?" he asked with an amused expression.

A flush climbed her face, but she nodded, savoring each new flavor that bathed her tongue, reveling in how the rich foods were complemented by the wine. Perry refilled her glass, seeming to enjoy watching her eat. She dabbed at her mouth with her napkin self-consciously.

"Try the dates," he said, picking one up with his fingers and offering it near her lips.

Her gaze locked with his and a plastic bubble seemed to descend over them, separating them from the rest of the diners. She hesitated, then opened her mouth and allowed him to place the morsel on her tongue. When she closed her mouth, her lips brushed the end of his finger, sending shockwaves of sexual awareness through her system. As she held the savory food on her tongue, Perry slowly pulled his hand back and licked his finger.

Her breasts grew heavy as she chewed the rich, salty date. When the sensory overload of Perry and their surroundings started to make her feel light-headed, she tore her gaze from his. Her heart pounded in her chest. If the man could make her feel this wanton over a meal, by the end of the weekend, she'd be a puddle of ooze.

Warning bells sounded in her head. The goal for the weekend was to have fun, not to fall head over heels in love with a playboy. Still, she had to admit that the idea of spending the weekend with Perry was a thousand times more appealing than hooking up with a stranger.

As the meal progressed and more food and wine was delivered to their table, Jane found herself warming toward Perry—in more places than her heart. Besides being so wonderful to look at with his dark hair and dark eyes and dark skin, he had a gift for conversation and for making her feel as if he were interested in her opinion. They talked about movies and politics, music and art. And she was surprised to learn that the playboy was well-read. It shouldn't have surprised her—he had, after all, passed the bar exam. But it was hard to reconcile the smooth, polished man sitting across from her with the man who'd answered his door shirtless and with his jeans half-unzipped.

Apparently, Nasty Boy had another side.

"Does your girlfriend know you're here?" she asked.

Perry blinked. "Girlfriend?"

"The woman I met and, um, *heard*."

"Oh, right. She's not my girlfriend, just a... friend."

"Ah." Friends with benefits.

He took another drink of wine and contemplated her as he swallowed. "So, Jane...have you been able to give my proposition some thought?"

She nodded and, liking the swimmy feeling it

gave her, kept nodding. "Although I think it's only fair that you know what you're getting into, Perry."

From the way his Adam's apple bobbed, she could tell she'd caught him off guard with her candor. "What am I getting into?"

Another large mouthful of wine warmed her throat as it went down, sending tendrils of alcohol curling through her limbs, further loosening her inhibitions, and her tongue. She felt reckless, and wanted to know what it felt like to do something...bad. "You should know that I came to Vegas to...unleash my inner wild child."

His eyebrows climbed. "Unleash your inner wild child?"

"In other words, to have a very...torrid...fling."

His mouth closed, then opened, and closed again, his eyes wide.

She smiled at his reaction, and strangely, it gave her courage. "Having second thoughts?"

"No," he said quickly. "No second thoughts."

But Jane knew what would put the bona fide ladies' man at ease. "As long as we both agree to no strings. When we get back to Atlanta, we'll go back to being…neighbors. Agreed?"

After a few seconds of charged silence, Perry lifted his wine glass to hers and she was gratified to see that the mischievous light had returned to his dark eyes. "Agreed."

11

As PERRY DRANK from his wine glass, he stared at the new and improved Jane Kurtz sitting across from him and conceded that he couldn't remember when he'd been more intrigued by a woman. Nor could he remember when he'd looked forward to the foreplay and the chase as much as the sex itself. One thing was sure—he intended to show Jane the time of her life...to safely guide her through the pleasures that Vegas had to offer, as well as the joys of the flesh that *he* had to offer.

And suddenly, he wanted to touch her.

"Let's dance," he said, nodding to the empty dance floor.

"I don't know how," she protested.

"I'll teach you." He stood and extended his hand

to pull her to her feet. "I thought you wanted to have fun," he challenged her.

She bit into her lip, then smiled and allowed him to lead her to the dance floor. He slid his arm to the curve of her waist and held her hand in his next to his shoulder.

"Stay on your toes and relax," he murmured in her ear. "Don't try to anticipate my movements, just follow my lead."

Still, she was stiff and awkward in his arms, glancing around self-consciously or staring at the floor. The woman had no idea what a swan she'd turned into, he realized. He was silent, taking simple, repetitive steps to the slow tempo, lightly caressing her back until she loosened and grew comfortable with his rhythm.

"You're a good dancer," she offered.

"My mother taught me. And my two sisters made me practice with them in the kitchen."

"You have sisters?"

"And two brothers."

"You're lucky," she said wistfully.

He nodded. "Do you have family near Atlanta?"

he asked, already knowing the answer and hating to make her say it.

"No. I don't have any family." She gave him a little smile. "I was a change-of-life baby, my parents were older. They've both been gone for a while now."

"I'm sorry," he said.

"Me, too. I keep thinking how happy they would be to know about me winning the lottery. How many things I could've given them."

He felt a tug on his heart. "You'll have it to spend on your own children, though."

The expression on her face was one of confusion. "I...guess so."

So she wasn't one of those women whose biological clock was ticking, he surmised. Did the thought of having children frighten her, or was she simply waiting for the right guy?

None of your business, Brewer, he told himself. *Don't go there*.

Gradually, he closed the space between them until their pelvises were pressed together. Then he moved his hips in time to the increased tempo and soon, she was mimicking his movements. He guessed she was an athlete—maybe a runner—with instinctive rhythm.

"You're a natural," he said with a happy grin.

The compliment buoyed her to smile and to put some extra movement in her steps. Perry swept her around the floor, his pulse throbbing higher. Being in sync on the dance floor was usually a good indication of chemistry in bed.

Plain Jane Kurtz was full of surprises.

Their intimate movements aligned all their erogenous zones. Perry gritted his teeth to keep his erection at bay, but under the influence of her beauty and her soft curves, nature would not be subdued. He knew the minute she became aware of his arousal from the startled look in her incredible blue eyes. But he wouldn't allow her to look away, pinning her down with his gaze. The woman came here to have a fling—she needed to know what she was getting herself into.

But she didn't shrink from his gaze, or from the intimate contact. If anything, she moved closer, sliding against his arousal ever so slightly as she moved to the music. Her response sent desire surging through his body. If he had his way, they'd go back to her room right now, hang a Do Not Disturb sign on the door, and not come up for air until Sunday around noon.

But he owed it to Jane to give her an experience different from what she would've had if she'd hooked up with some horny guy at the bar. Wasn't that why he'd followed her out here, to protect her?

So when the song ended, he held her close for a heartbeat, then slowly unwound her body from his and led her back to the table. His heart was thumping, but more from the proximity to Jane than from the exertion. Her happy smile lit her entire face, putting a sparkle in her eyes that he'd never seen, not even when he'd congratulated her on winning the lottery.

A pang struck his chest—apparently Jane Kurtz hadn't experienced very many truly happy moments, moments when she forgot herself and laughed with abandon. And knowing that he'd put that smile on her face did something to his stomach. He suddenly had the feeling that he was playing with fire. But when he helped her into her chair and got an inadvertent glimpse down her bright pink blouse at her lacy black bra, he decided that he wouldn't mind going down in flames.

They finished the wine in their glasses and he signaled for the check, hesitating only a second before signing his room number to the slightly enormous bill. He was pushing the limits on his credit cards, but if everything turned out with the Kendall case, he'd be okay.

"Shall we go lose some money to the house?" he asked with a grin.

She nodded eagerly, and they left the restaurant, with her leaning into him more readily than only a few hours ago. Good—she was growing more comfortable around him. A blip of panic darted through his chest at the possibility that Jane might fall for him, but he chastised himself for the ego-tistical thought. After all, Jane was the one who'd insisted on the no-strings condition.

"What's your pleasure?" he asked as they entered the grand casino, abuzz with people and lights and the ringing of bells from the slots area.

Jane looked around, her face alight with curiosity. To his irritation, as she contemplated their surroundings, he saw lots of men's heads turn in her direction to contemplate *her*.

"I want to try everything," she said, clasping his arm. "Will you teach me, Perry?"

One look into those animated big blue eyes and he was utterly lost. "That's why I'm here." Besides, he was hoping to win enough at the craps table to actually pay for some of this trip.

She grinned. "Slots first?"

"Sure, that's easy. Let's get some coins."

Jane reached into her purse and pulled out rolls of quarters and dollars. "I have some."

Well, that answered the quarters or condoms question, he realized steering her in the direction of a slot machine on the end of a row.

"The machines near foot traffic tend to have a higher payout," he said. "If customers see people winning, they're more likely to play themselves."

Jane settled on the stool, oblivious to the fact that her mini-skirt had hiked up on her toned thighs, giving him an inadvertent flash of pink panties. His cock twitched and he wondered how he was going to get through the evening with this woman who had no idea how hot she was. Averting his gaze, he maneuvered to stand behind her and explained how to select the buttons to play the various games.

"Then you just feed it coins and pull the lever. The machine will tell you if you've won."

She began cramming in coins and pulling the lever as fast as she could, her face flushed with excitement.

"Whoa," he said with a laugh. "You might want to slow down. You need to pace yourself…"

She gave him a withering look. "Perry, I just won the lottery, remember?"

"Oh. Right."

Good thing, too, considering she ran through all of her rolls of coins in record time. But she loved every minute of it, he conceded as she slid down from the stool in a way that confirmed her pink panties were edged in black lace.

He bit the inside of his cheek and led her to a beginner blackjack table, where she promptly lost more money with more enthusiasm than anyone he'd ever seen. For the next hour and a half, they went from the roulette wheel to the poker tables, to the craps table, where he lost a small fortune trying to teach her how to play, then watched her happily lose a small fortune, too. All the while she sipped on an endless glass of wine and proceeded to drive him crazy by easing against his body with more and more familiarity.

Toward the end, she got on a roll at the craps table and proceeded to win back her losses. He, on the other hand, was in too deep to try to recoup. But everyone at the table got caught up in Jane's gusto—and her cleavage—and cheered her on, raking in their winnings after every roll.

Every time she leaned over the table to toss the dice, she backed into him, tucking her shapely rear against his cock, which seemed to be operating on a spring tonight. When his arousal met her resistance, she pressed back harder, filling his head with images of pulling her skirt up and her panties down and taking her right there, heedless of the crowd. At this point, he probably wouldn't last longer than a schoolboy anyway.

By the time her luck ran out, he was gritting his teeth against the lust pumping through his body, and ready to punch the guys standing around giving him knowing glances.

"What now?" Jane asked, turning around and smiling up at him with the fervor and fuzziness of a coed who'd had a little too much to drink.

He wet his lips. "What did you have in mind?"

She held up the cash she'd won. "Let's go to a show."

His erection shrank as he envisioned taking in a lounge act. "What kind of show?"

Jane walked over to a rack of brochures sitting against the wall and plucked one from its slot, then walked back and handed it to him. "This kind of show."

Perry glanced at the full color brochure and his eyes widened. "A male strip club?"

She lifted her hands. "I've never been to one."

"Neither have I," he said dryly.

"It sounds like fun."

He begged to differ. When he'd told her he'd show her a good time, taking her to ogle other naked men hadn't been in his plans.

"Will you take me?" Jane asked, batting her lashes and reminding him that this weekend was all about her needs, not his.

With resignation, Perry shrugged. "Sure."

12
___

WHEN PERRY HAD fantasized about Jane's thighs pressing against his ears, he hadn't imagined she would be sitting on his shoulders, waving a ten dollar bill at a shirtless fireman dancing on stage and screaming, "Take it off!"

Gyrating to the pulsing music, the buff man waved his red hard hat at her, then in one motion, ripped off his pants, revealing a thong with flames shooting up from the crotch. Perry rolled his eyes but the crowd near the stage went wild, Jane included, lurching forward with such momentum that he had to shift abruptly to keep them both from toppling.

He was pretty sure the woman had consumed more alcohol than her body had ever processed before. He was doing his part to keep her on her feet—so to speak—by making her eat breadsticks and nachos to absorb the vodka in the green apple martinis she'd been tossing back.

After all, he had a vested interest in keeping her conscious. After nursing a hard-on for most of the evening, he was hoping to spend the night in her bed.

But damn if it didn't hurt his pride just a little to know that Fred the Fireman was priming the pump.

"Take it *all* off!" she shouted, waving her fist in the air.

Fred strutted up and down the stage a few seconds longer to whip the crowd into a frenzy, then stopped in front of Jane and pointed to a string on his thong for her to pull.

Perry frowned and straightened—that was a little bold, and he was sure Jane would refuse.

But to his amazement, she reached forward and plucked at the string, relieving the man of the last scrap of fabric that separated the audience from his, uh, hose.

The crowd went wild, but Perry could only stare at the man's penis with bewilderment. He was getting *paid* to wag that beanie-weenie?

"Woo-hoo!" Jane yelled, squeezing Perry's ears. "Shake that thang!"

He winced, holding on to her knees. After Cal the Construction worker, Jantzen the Jungle guy, and Fred the Fireman, he wasn't sure he could stand another session of a costumed dude coming out on the runway and shaking his *thang* at a room full of women and gay men (present company excluded) to some lame disco tune.

"About ready to call it a night?" he shouted up to Jane.

She leaned forward until her hair fell over his face, her upside down face nose to nose with him. "Already?"

"'Fraid so," he said, straining to stay upright under her gymnastics. He crouched to lower her close enough to the floor to dismount clumsily. When he stood, he rubbed his ringing ears, then hurried to tug down her skirt that was rucked up around her waist. She was too busy tossing dollar bills at naked Fred to notice. "Bye, Fred! Bye!"

Perry shepherded her outside and into a cab, then fell back against the seat, exhausted.

"Wasn't that fun?" she asked, bouncing.

"Sure," he said.

Jane frowned. "You didn't like it?"

"Uh, watching men take off their clothes isn't my favorite thing to do, Jane."

"Be a sport. There were lots of other guys there."

"News flash, dollface, they were gay."

Her eyebrows flew up. "Really?"

"Really."

She covered her mouth and laughed, then sobered. "Did you just call me dollface?"

"I did." He picked up her hand. "I'm glad you had fun tonight."

She giggled, a lilting sound that did funny things to his stomach. "The night's not over," she said in a sing-songy voice.

Perry smiled and pulled her closer, then pushed his hands into her silky hair and curled his fingers around her neck. How long had he wanted to do that?

"You're beautiful," he murmured before pulling her lips to his. He half expected her to resist, but she didn't, flicking her tongue out to taste him before opening her mouth to his. Then she went on the offensive, slashing her mouth over his and stabbing her tongue against his, deepening the kiss with bites and moans. Before he realized what was happening, she twisted in the seat to straddle him.

Perry groaned—relief and anticipation to finally have her in his arms warred with the knowledge that the cabbie was weaving in the street trying to get an eyeful. So even as Perry's hands slid down to the warm bare skin exposed by her inadequate skirt, he wanted to shield her from the other man's voyeuristic eyes. And as much as he wanted to have sex with her right now—this instant, in fact— he reminded himself that he'd followed Jane so she could spend the weekend with someone different from the guys who would hump her in a cab.

"Whoa," he said, pulling back and easing her off his lap while he still could.

"Did I do something wrong?" she asked.

"No," he said quickly, pulling his hand down his face. "Please, hold that thought." Then he knocked on the Plexiglass divider to get the cabbie's attention. "Hey, buddy, step on it, would you?" He kissed

Jane again—this time more slowly and sweetly, then he put his arm around her shoulder and held her against him, willing the taxi to take flight.

JANE'S HEAD was spinning by the time they reached her hotel room door. She was still a little woozy from the alcohol, but mostly from being with Perry all evening—the dinner, the dancing, the gambling, then the strip club, and throughout, the underlying flirtation between them building... accumulating...mushrooming...

Her face burned when she thought of pressing her body against his arousal at every chance, of wrapping her legs around his head to sit on his shoulders at the club, of straddling him in the taxi. Each encounter had set her on fire.

But it was when he had pulled her off his lap and tucked her head into his shoulder that things had felt...wrong. Because in that moment she had realized that it would be too easy to fall for this surprising, sexy man. And now she was having second thoughts about that torrid affair, because she didn't want to develop strings...

He helped her with the door key, reminding her of the morning after he'd said those things about her, when she couldn't see the lock because her eyes were scratchy and swollen from crying and because she'd been wearing those stupid sunglasses. At that moment, she hadn't wanted him to be nice, hadn't wanted him to apologize, because it was easier to think that he was a jerk than to think that he was human. Easier to dislike him than to…like him.

The door swung open into her suite, and even though the room was beautifully furnished with sofa, chairs, tables, wardrobes, and electronics, her gaze was drawn to the king-size bed like a laser. Her pulse picked up and her chest itched from a sudden nerve rash. When he stepped up behind her and pulled her hair back to lower a kiss on her neck, she panicked.

"Perry," she said, turning to face him.

The erotic look in his deep brown eyes, the sensual curve of his mouth almost stopped her… the man was devastatingly handsome, and she had proof through her own walls that he was a great lover. Being made love to by this man would no doubt be a physical revelation, but she needed to put some emotional distance between them in her head.

"I had a great time tonight," she continued, "but maybe this is all happening too fast."

He swallowed hard, then nodded and stepped back.

"I mean, we still have tomorrow," she said quickly. "And…tomorrow night."

Perry kept nodding. "Right." He cleared his throat. "Tomorrow then."

She stepped to the doorway. "Where are you staying?"

He pointed to the door next to hers. "Right here. A favor from the desk clerk." He gave her a crooked smile. "Goodnight."

"Goodnight," she murmured, then slowly closed the door and leaned against it with a sigh.

It had been the most fun, exciting night of her life. Never in her wildest dreams had she imagined spending the weekend with someone as handsome and sexy as Perry Brewer. She walked into the bathroom, slipping off her sandals along the way. She paused in front of the vanity mirror to remove her earrings, then stared at her unfamiliar reflection.

The stylists at the salon had worked miracles, coaxing a sexy beauty from the depths of a plain Jane. The hair made the biggest difference, she conceded. Who knew she could carry off the whitest platinum blond? And even though she'd tidied lots of brows herself, she wouldn't have believed that waxing and arching her own brows would have opened up her eyes so dramatically and given her face an almost exotic expression.

And neither would she have believed that a simple sexy outfit would have uncovered her figure, and given her the confidence to flirt. She pulled the silky fuchsia-colored blouse from the waistband of the mini-skirt and unbuttoned it, revealing the most decadent black lace bra she'd ever seen, much less owned. She unzipped the skirt and stepped out of it, revealing the black edged hip-hugging pink panties. She'd spent a week's salary on the bra and panty set alone.

Such a shame that no one would see them.

She sighed and donned a short black robe, fastening the tie around her waist. Then she padded back into the bedroom and glanced at the clock. 1:30 a.m. Ten minutes ago she'd convinced herself she was ready to go to bed…alone. But now—

A noise caught her attention and she turned her head, then realized it had come from the other side of the wall, from Perry's room. He was still awake—was he restless? Regretting the fact that he'd followed her here? Laughing to himself that she hadn't been able to back up her bold words about having a torrid affair?

Snatches of the sounds of his lovemaking that had penetrated her condo walls came back to her…the woman shouting things, being driven out of control… But there had been no noises from Perry—had his mouth been occupied?

She swallowed hard. The image of Perry's head between her own legs tonight while she sat on his shoulders at the club had been erotic enough. But the thought of his mouth at the juncture of her thighs sent moisture pooling there. No man had ever made love to her that way.

She picked up a drinking glass and held it to the wall, then put her ear to the end, wondering if it conducted sound like she'd seen in the movies.

It did…some. She could hear him moving around, his footsteps, and a thud—him falling into bed? The low murmur of conversation—the television, perhaps…or him talking on the telephone? The vision of him sprawled on his bed, his long limbs bare and brown, made her midsection tighten with desire. Was he a boxer man, or a briefs man? Or did he sleep in the nude?

Jane lowered the glass, her chest rising and falling rapidly. She thought she'd be more prepared to have sex with Perry by waiting another day, but what if the chemistry that they'd experienced today was gone tomorrow? Could she really expect it to get better than it had been tonight? After all, they were both ripe for each other *now*.

With her heart in her throat, she set down the glass and padded to her door. Then before she could change her mind, she grabbed her room key, opened her door and walked out into the hall to rap on Perry's door.

A few seconds passed, then the door swung open, revealing Perry in hastily donned slacks, considering they were zipped, but not buttoned. "Jane, is something wrong?"

Seeing his expanse of muscled chest reminded her of the first time she'd knocked on his door, and old self-doubts threatened to tie her tongue. But hadn't she come to Vegas to unleash her inner wild child? To do something…bad?

"I changed my mind," she said, sounding stronger than she felt. "D-do you mind if I come in?"

Realization dawned on Perry's face, followed by a slow, sexy smile. He reached for her hand and pulled her inside, stopping only to hang a Do Not Disturb sign on the knob before he closed the door.

13

To Jane, the click of Perry's door closing was like a gong sounding the end to her staid, dull existence. His room was dimly lit, the bed covers slightly rumpled. A thumping rock tune played on the stereo. It was as if she literally had crossed a threshold from good girl to…bad.

When Perry turned to look at her with hungry eyes, a shiver passed over her shoulders.

But it felt *soooo* good.

He came to her and lowered his mouth to hers for a kiss that went from warm to scorching in a heartbeat. For some reason, he seemed obsessed with her hair, sinking his hands into it and caressing the nape of her neck while he devoured her mouth. Then he pulled back, his hands dropping to the tie on her robe.

When the robe fell open and off her shoulders, any panic or shyness she might have felt from standing in front of him in her underwear was overridden by his groan of pleasure as his warm hands closed in around her waist. He lifted her, half-walking, half-carrying her to his bed, kissing her collarbone and shoulders, sending waves of pleasure over her entire body.

The man had already surpassed her previous lovers, and he'd barely touched her. She sank into the softness of his pillows, the anticipation of what was to come rendering her breathless. He stood by the bed and stepped out of his slacks, answering the boxers or briefs question—white athletic-style briefs hugged his powerful thighs and dipped low enough on his narrow waist to reveal the tip of his impressive erection, already shiny with need.

The thought of him inside her made her languid and malleable. His bigness, his maleness, was overwhelming. She remembered thinking when she first saw him that his long, hard body appeared to be made for sex, and she realized now that she was right—everything about him called to a woman. She felt her body readying for him, and wanted to be rid of the scraps of fabric between them. She reached for the front hook of her bra and unfastened it, allowing her breasts to spill forward, their tips distended and eager for his touch.

His face darkened with desire as he climbed on top of her. "You're beautiful," he breathed against her skin, then captured one peak in his warm, wet mouth.

She sighed and arched into him, unprepared for the onslaught of erotic sensations as his body seemingly stroked hers from head to toe. Every inch of his skin presented new textures and temperatures—warm, hot, soft, firm, hard, rough.

Jane threaded her fingers through his thick, dark hair and moaned as he drew on her nipple.

"Tell me what you want, Jane," he whispered. "Tell me what feels good."

The idea shocked her, but somehow it felt natural with Perry. "It feels good when you kiss my breasts."

He lowered a few chaste kisses to her cleavage. "Like that?"

A flush warmed her cheeks. "Kiss…my nipples."

"Kiss?" he asked, placing open mouthed kisses all around her plump nipples. "Or lick?"

"Lick," she murmured, moaned when his tongue teased the turgid peaks.

"Lick?" he asked. "Or bite?"

She gasped when he took the nipple between his teeth and applied light pressure. She bucked when the sensation arrowed directly to her core. "Yes… oh, yes."

He moaned his pleasure, too, his tongue vibrating against her skin.

She skimmed her hands over the smooth, muscled expanse of his back, then down the indentation of his spine, and under the waistband of his briefs to clasp his firm buttocks. He groaned and rocked his pelvis against hers with the promise of future delights, then started his descent down her body, kissing his way along her stomach while kneading her breasts.

When she realized his destination, she tensed, unsure of what to expect.

"Easy," he said against her navel, lifting her hips to ease off the pink and black panties. "I'd never hurt you, Jane."

She tried to relax, but her body was too preoccupied with new revelations. He dropped kisses and licks on her thighs, going back and forth, finally urging her knees open to allow him access to the jewel of her desire. When the air hit her wet folds, she closed her eyes, unable to bear him looking at her so intimately. But when his mouth closed over the tiny sensitive nub, she dug her heels into the bed and cried out, whipping her head back and forth. The torture was too exquisite—she couldn't bear it.

But she couldn't bear for him to stop, either.

So she lay helpless while he made love to her with his mouth, aware of the orgasm stirring in her womb, swirling round and round, gathering centrifugal force as his tongue stroked her longer and harder.

She undulated against his mouth, thrashing against the mattress when her limbs reached sensory overload. Again and again he stoked her fire, higher and higher until her climax rocketed to the surface and broke all over her body in tiny little pieces. She shouted his name and her pleasure, vocalizing the erotic earthquake he'd unleashed in her.

As her body pulsed with recovery, she clawed at his back to bring them face to face. He kissed her hard, giving her a shocking taste of herself that clung to his mouth.

She pushed at the waistband of his briefs, using hands, then feet to drag them down and off his long legs. She clasped his thick erection, reveling in the velvety smoothness and the throbbing strength.

"You're killing me," he murmured.

"I want you inside me," she whispered, unable to wait any longer.

At the sound of her raspy request, Perry almost came on the spot. The woman had had him on a slow burn for hours, and he wasn't sure how much more he could stand. He wanted to drive himself inside her and stay there for hours, but at this point, he'd be lucky to get the condom on.

He pulled away from her long enough to reach for his wallet on the nightstand to withdraw a foil packet, then set his jaw while he sheathed himself.

With a deep breath for restraint, he settled into the cradle of her wet thighs. His heat sought hers, the tip of his cock pressing against her opening. He kissed her again, trying to postpone the moment, but lust surged through his body. The idea of loving her slowly and gently vanished as he thrust inside her slick channel with one powerful stroke.

She gasped, and the feeling of her sex absorbing his took his breath, too. He nuzzled her neck, allowing them both to become accustomed to the sensation of their bodies joined together.

With the first stroke, he knew he wouldn't last long. She was so tight, it was as if she were trying to consume him. This woman, he realized as his breathing became more ragged, was dangerous…more dangerous than any of the hell-raisers he'd bedded. A good girl capable of doing bad things…Christ, that was a powerful combination.

To his astonishment, he realized from her spasms and her escalating moans that she was on the verge of another orgasm. A heartbeat later, she bit down on his shoulder to muffle her cries of ecstasy. Perry felt his own orgasm being wrenched from his body, as if she were taking it from him.

His body contracted violently with the most mind-numbing release of his life.

Afterward, Perry gently rolled to her side, too stunned to talk. Fortunately, within seconds, Jane had fallen into an exhausted sleep. He turned his head to watch her chest rise and fall, perplexed and disturbed at these…feelings that seemed to be plaguing him.

A torrid affair, they'd agreed. No strings. For the rest of the weekend, he had to make sure their affair was more about having sex and less about making…love.

Suddenly a smile curved his mouth. If little Jane Kurtz wanted torrid, he'd show her torrid.

_14_

WHEN JANE JERKED awake, she was utterly disoriented, her heart thumping wildly. The room was dark, and an unfamiliar warmth lay next to her.

A man, whose hand was curled over her breast.

Perry Brewer.

She closed her eyes and it all came rushing back—the flirtatious evening, the goodnight at her hotel room door, her trek to his room, their incredible lovemaking.

Correction—the incredible _sex_.

She turned her head gingerly to study his sleeping profile in the thin light streaming in from the bathroom, and to her dismay, her heart flipped over. She couldn't start thinking that this physical relationship meant anything to Perry other than a chance to settle some chest-thumping score in his mind, to prove to her that he was a nice guy.

A nice guy with a tongue that wouldn't quit.

Her toes curled as the memories of what he'd done to her came back full force…along with the urge to flee. She didn't have experience with men like Perry, but she knew the best way to maintain an emotional distance was to avoid intimate morning-after situations.

So she inched her way out of bed, holding her breath when his hand fell from her breast to the mattress. But other than a slight interruption in his breathing, Perry didn't stir. Holding her aching head and wincing at the sore muscles in her hips and legs, she felt around the floor, looking for her clothes.

She found her bra and the robe, which had her room key in the pocket and when he shifted in the bed, she decided to sacrifice her panties and vamoose. After shrugging into the robe, she tied the belt, cast one last glance at Perry's long nude body tangled in the sheets, and let herself out as quietly as possible. In the brightly lit hallway, she squinted and averted her gaze from the passing couple who offered sly smiles in her direction.

An embarrassed flush climbed her face—she never thought she'd be sneaking out of a man's hotel room in the middle of the night wearing only her robe.

But she had, she realized as she ducked into her own room, officially unleashed her inner wild child. She stretched tall on her toes and reached overhead in a yawn that gave way to a quiet little squeal of pleasure as she hugged herself.

Last night had been…magical. When Perry had thrust his body into hers, she thought she might come undone. She'd never experienced a physical connection like that with any man.

And they still had another day—and night— together.

She smiled to herself, then pushed her hair out of her face and went in search of an aspirin. A painkiller and a shower later, she fell into her own bed and curled beneath the covers. Her body was exhausted, but her mind didn't seem to want to shut down.

She kept replaying moments from the previous

night that had surprised her—how he'd gone out of his way to make sure she'd had fun, even at a male strip club. How he'd been willing to walk away from a night of sex because at first she'd been uncomfortable. How he'd taken great care to give her pleasure before he took any of his own.

Jane rolled over on her back and stared at the ceiling. She had to do something to ward off these unbidden feelings of...*affection* she was developing for Perry. After all, every woman who left his bed probably felt special afterward. It was all part of his routine. So to get through the rest of the weekend with her heart intact, she'd have to avoid those private little moments—the stolen kisses, the cuddling—that made her imagination spin out of control.

She'd focus on the sex—the hot, molten sex that she'd come here for, the kind of slam sex that only two people with absolutely no ties could truly enjoy.

A knock at her door startled her. She glanced at the clock. It was only 4:30 a.m., way too early for housecleaning. Maybe someone had reported her lurking around in the hallway. She snatched up her robe, walked to the door, and looked through the peephole.

Perry.

Her heart bounced crazily as she opened the door.

He was dressed in rumpled jeans and a T-shirt, and his hair and skin were damp. A lazy grin curled his mouth. "Hi."

"Hi," she whispered.

"I took a shower."

"So did I."

He scanned her from wet hair to pink polished toes. "So you're naked under that robe?"

She nodded.

He looked right, then left, then back to her. "Well, I won't say I've never had sex in a hotel hallway, but unless you want to add it to your repertoire, maybe I should come in."

Jane grinned, and they were kissing before the door closed.

"I woke up with a perfectly good hard-on," he murmured, "and you were gone."

She untied her robe and let it drop to the floor. "Oh, no."

His eyes lit up as he lifted his T-shirt over his head and unzipped his pants. "Oh, yes."

When he was naked, too, he caught her mouth in an explosive kiss and walked her backward to the bed, his erection jutting into her bare stomach. He eased her back onto the bed and climbed on top of her, nuzzling her breasts. But feeling bold, she rolled him over and straddled him, eager to try her hand at pleasing him the way he'd pleased her.

Perry didn't object.

She clasped his rigid cock and stroked him slowly and purposefully until the velvety head was lubricated and shiny. He moaned his pleasure and massaged her breasts, his eyes hooded with desire. His response gave her the nerve to take him into her mouth. At his sharp intake of breath, female satisfaction flowed through her.

After a few seconds, she lifted her head. "Tell me what you like."

"You're doing fine," he said, gasping.

"Seriously," she said. "Do you like it when I do this?" She licked the head of his cock like a lollipop.

"Yes," he hissed.

"And this?" She took in his length as far as her throat would allow and caressed his soft sack.

"Yesssss."

"And this?" She sucked on the tip, swirling her tongue around the ridge.

His eyes were nearly closed, his face contorted with pleasure-pain. "God, yes."

Taking her cues from his movements and noises, she explored his sex thoroughly with her mouth, then pulled away long enough to remove a condom from her purse.

"My treat this time," she said to his raised-eyebrow expression.

She tore open the package with her teeth, then carefully rolled on the condom. Feeling wicked and totally wanton, she straddled his erection and slowly lowered her body onto his while he palmed her breasts. The fullness of him inside her at this angle was complete.

A muscle worked in Perry's jaw, but as if he understood how deeply he had penetrated her, he allowed her to control the movement. At first she could only contract around him, then her strokes were short and slow. But when she became accustomed to his size, she found a rhythm that gave them both optimum pleasure. He reached down to gently massage her clit with his thumb, and she leaned her head back to enjoy the erotic ride.

She came first, but her writhing and bucking carried him over the edge with her. He held on to her waist, his body bowing in his guttural release to the point that he lifted her off the bed with him.

When their spasms had slowed, Jane fell forward onto the soft mat of dark hair on his chest, listening to the soothing, strong beat of his heart as she drifted off to sleep.

No, she wasn't falling in love with this man. It was only sex…no strings…

15

"ARE YOU GOING to quit your job?" Perry asked.

Jane shrugged. They were lounging over a luxurious room service breakfast in her bed. "I guess so. It wouldn't make much sense for me to work."

"It would if you love your job," he said quietly. "Do you?"

His seriousness caught her off guard. She shifted awkwardly in the towel she was wearing. "I enjoy it, although some days it seems frivolous. I make people look good so they can go on camera to talk about things like how to decorate a pet's bedroom."

He smiled and shrugged. "It's entertainment. It makes people happy. We have to have that in the world, don't we?"

She nodded. "But now that I have the means, I'd

like to do something to truly make a difference in the world." Jane winced. "Does that sound cheesy?"

"Not at all. It sounds very admirable."

Her gaze locked with his and all the moisture left her mouth. How could being astride this man naked be more comfortable than a simple conversation about her job?

Just another reminder that she needed to keep things…carnal.

Her cell phone rang. She leaned over to fish it from her purse and glanced at the screen. It was Eve.

"I should get this," she said to Perry.

"I'll take a shower," he offered, then headed toward her bathroom.

Jane pushed the incoming call button. "Good morning," she said cheerfully.

"It's already noon here," Eve said. "You must be having a great time. I've been calling and calling."

Panic blipped in her chest. "Is something wrong?"

"Only that my best friend is acting like someone I don't know, going off to Vegas, doing God knows what."

"It's your fault," Jane said, popping a grape into her mouth.

"How?"

"The show you did with Bette Valentine on unleashing your inner wild child. I guess it spoke to me."

Eve choked out a laugh. "Jane, you don't *have* an inner wild child." Then she sobered. "Do you?"

Perry came padding back into the bedroom, cock swinging. "You're out of towels," he said, snatching the one she had wrapped around her.

"Is that a man's voice?" Eve asked.

"Yes," Jane said, enjoying the view of him leaving the room and stepping into the glass shower stall.

"You met a guy?"

She was distracted by the sight of Perry leaning his head back under the shower head and soaping his long, powerful body. Her own body was tender and sore but, incredibly, she wanted him again.

"Jane, are you there?"

"Yeah, sorry. Actually, it's someone I already knew."

"Who?"

"My neighbor."

"Your neighbor, the jerk? You went to Vegas with *him?*"

The water ran off his shoulders like a waterfall cascading off a rock cliff. Jane wet her lips. "Uh, no. He kind of followed me. It's a long story."

Eve made a rueful noise in her throat. "I'm worried about you, Jane. What do you know about this guy?"

"Enough."

"*Enough?* Someone has kidnapped my level-headed friend Jane and replaced her with an imposter! What's this guy's name?"

Jane laughed. "Perry Brewer. He's an attorney."

Perry looked up and saw her watching him, then smiled and crooked his finger.

"Sorry, Eve. Gotta go."

"But Jane—"

"I'll call you." She disconnected the call, then stood and walked to the shower, her breasts heavy with need, her nipples stiff. She slipped inside and channeled her fingers through the sudsy dark hair on his wide chest, heaving a sigh. "What do you say we go shopping later?"

"Later," he agreed, rounding his hands over her buttocks with a groan. "Much later."

PERRY STOOD in the lobby waiting for Jane, his phone pressed to his ear. "I realize my credit card is over the limit," he said to the representative on the phone, "but I've been a customer for a long time. Can't you make an exception?"

"I'm sorry, sir. We can't extend your credit limit until we receive a payment."

He pulled a hand down his face. "If I could afford to make a payment, I wouldn't need an extension on my limit, now, would I?"

"I'm sorry, sir."

He sighed. "It's not your fault. Thank you." Perry closed his phone and tamped down his irritation. He still had an emergency card or two, but if he didn't win the Kendall case, or if the damages were smaller than his client deserved, he'd be digging himself and the firm out of debt far into the foreseeable future.

"No good deed goes unpunished," he murmured. When Jane appeared on the other side of the lobby, he couldn't help but smile. Take this little Good Samaritan jaunt, for instance.

He'd traveled here to keep sweet little Jane Kurtz from doing something she'd regret, and now he was on the offensive. They'd both agreed to a no-strings affair, but he was growing attached to her…a doomed emotion, he knew, because he had no intention of being anyone's boyfriend, and had no desire to be monogamous.

Monogamous—hmm. While Jane chatted with the concierge, an idea occurred to him.

He called directory assistance and after a couple of dead ends, found a company who could fulfill his request. Feeling much better about the direction of their torrid affair, he walked over to where she stood, fresh and lovely in a sexy yellow dress and sandals. When she saw him, her face broke into a smile that hit him like a punch to the spleen.

"Ready to go shopping?" he asked.

She nodded happily.

"Where to? Clothing, jewelry, car lots?"

"Electronics. I'd like an MP3 player."

He raised his eyebrows. "That's all? I thought you were unleashing your inner wild child this weekend."

Jane laughed. "I might look around."

Checking his watch, he said, "We have two hours."

"What's happening in two hours?"

"That, my little wild child, is a surprise."

She looked intrigued, but didn't ask any questions. She trusted him. She'd trusted him from the beginning, he realized.

Even after he'd given her reason not to, with his thoughtless remarks about her looks.

That bothered him a little, only because he wasn't sure he was worthy of her trust. He wanted to chastise her, but how could he do that without making himself look bad?

Perry pinched the bridge of his nose. He wasn't thinking straight—the woman had drained him physically with that sleeper bod of hers that wouldn't quit...and wouldn't let him quit.

"Are you okay?" Jane asked.

"Fine," he said, hailing a taxi.

"You don't have to go with me."

"Hey, if there's one place a man doesn't mind to shop, it's in an electronics store."

She seemed pacified and blissfully unaware of the turmoil he was going through on the short cab ride. He would be fine once they got back to Atlanta, he reasoned. Once they went back to being neighbors.

At the electronics shop, Jane was like a kid in a candy store. At his urging, she bought an MP3 player and a few accessories, several CDs, a digital camera, and a top of the line digital video camera.

"Why not?" he asked.

"I don't exactly have the lottery money yet," she said, biting her lip.

"But soon?"

"We're all supposed to receive wires later this week."

He smiled. "I think you'll be okay."

"I hope so. Or else not only will I have to keep my job, but I'll have to get a second one."

She was caught between being conservative and optimistic, he realized on the cab ride to their secret destination. All her life she'd probably yearned to do something wild, but something—her upbringing, her self-doubts, had held her in check. Letting go this weekend was undoubtedly a huge leap for her…and she still was afraid to believe she had the world at her fingertips.

It made him want to give it to her.

To derail his baffling train of thought, Perry removed the video camera from the box to show her how to use it. Then he turned it on her. "Wave at the camera, Jane."

She waved, but looked self-conscious and averted her glance.

"Don't look away," he chided. "The camera loves you, Jane."

His offhand words hung in the air awkwardly, and he wished he could take them back. Her face underwent a myriad of emotions. Confusion? Apprehension? Hope?

Perry swallowed hard, cursing his slip, relieved when he realized that the cab had slowed to a halt.

"Where are we?" Jane asked, looking out the window.

Perry paid the driver and helped her out with all her packages. "I scheduled us for a massage."

She smiled. "That sounds wonderful."

"A couple's massage. Together, in the same room, if that's okay with you."

She nodded. "Sure."

"You'll have a male masseuse, and I'll have a female."

"Okay."

"We'll be naked…and so will they."

16

WHEN PERRY'S WORDS sank in, a little thrill of apprehension and anticipation ran through her. "We'll all be naked?"

"Only if that's okay with you."

She felt gauche and naive. "Will there be…?"

"No sex on the premises. Just touching. It's a regular massage, but we'll be able to see each other…and watch."

Her sex tingled.

"And," he said, clasping her hand, "if at any time you feel uncomfortable, just let me know and we'll leave."

"Okay. But I want to pay for my half."

"It's my treat," he said in a voice that brooked no argument. "After all, I crashed your plans to have a torrid affair—I wouldn't want you to go home disappointed."

That wasn't likely to happen, she thought. Being with Perry had already blown her expectations out of the water.

He held the door for her and she walked into the luxurious lobby, hoping her face wasn't as red as it felt. She glanced around at the other people waiting—some single women, some single men, some couples—and wondered if they were all there for a similar experience.

What a sheltered life she'd led.

"They do regular spa treatments here, too," Perry whispered, as if he'd read her mind. "It's a legitimate business."

"So you've been here before?"

"No. But I checked it out."

His response pleased her because she had doubted that she could do or share anything sexually with the playboy that he hadn't experienced before.

They walked up to the receptionist's desk and Perry gave his name for the appointment. After a short wait, they were led to a private changing room with a shower and a locker to store their packages and belongings. Two immaculate white robes hung on hooks, and two sets of flip flops sat on the floor. Soft Asian music played overhead.

With her pulse thumping wildly, Jane disrobed, aware of Perry's gaze on her as he did the same. She stepped into the shower for a quick rinse, and he joined her, intertwining their fingers to hold her at arm's length while warm water spilled over them. His erection jutted forward, prodding her stomach, but as if by mutual agreement, they only kissed before emerging.

Still, her body was singing with awareness as they donned the soft robes and slipped their feet into the flimsy grass sandals.

"Ready?" he asked.

She nodded.

"Are you sure?"

Feeling breathless, she brought his hand to her chest to feel her heart pounding. "I'm excited."

His eyes darkened with desire, then he opened the door leading to the massage room. Inside, the lighting in the aqua-colored room was dim and mellow. Two sheet-covered platforms were situated about three feet apart. The music was slightly louder here, the air permeated with the scent of grasses and musk.

Following his lead, she removed her robe and lay face-down on one of the platforms, draping a folded towel over her bare bottom.

"It's nice," she said, already feeling relaxed.

"I'm glad you like it so far," he said, reaching out to her. "Remember, let me know if you want to stop."

She nodded and pressed her palm against his.

A quiet rap sounded at the door, then a beautiful, slender woman with dark hair and a handsome, muscular blond man entered quietly, both of them dressed in short robes. They murmured a quiet greeting, but were otherwise silent as they prepared a tray of scented oils.

Perry winked at her and she inhaled deeply of the scented air, trying to relax despite the sexual energy in the air.

Still dressed, their masseuses began at the same

time, positioning themselves next to the platforms in a way that allowed her and Perry to maintain eye contact.

When the man's oiled hands first touched her shoulders, she tensed, then gave in to the gentle, but firm ministrations. On the other platform, Perry's masseuse was working her magic on his back muscles.

The man worked his way down her spine, using his palms, fingers, and knuckles to apply pressure that stimulated her muscles, then coaxed them to quiet. When he reached her buttocks, he removed the towel quietly, rendering her completely nude. The woman had done the same thing to Perry, and just the sight of his long, naked body caused Jane's midsection to tighten. He was eyeing her body just as hungrily.

The man re-oiled his hands with a sandalwood lotion, then began to massage her buttocks and thighs with long, purposeful strokes. Twice he brushed her inner thighs, sending a pleasant rush of moisture there. Then he moved to her calves and feet. Both masseuses spent a long time on the soles of their clients' feet and Jane hadn't realized before what a turn on it could be.

"Turn over, please," her masseuse murmured in her ear, and she heard the woman tell Perry the same thing.

Jane turned over, fully exposed to the blonde man's appreciative gaze. While she and Perry were getting settled, both the man and the woman quietly removed their robes.

Jane's thighs tingled. It was the sheer sight of all the naked skin that felt so taboo. The woman was beautiful—her breasts small, but firm and tilted, with plump, pink nipples. She was tanned all over, with a trim triangle of dark hair at the juncture of her thighs.

The man was equally beautiful, his muscular body tanned and hairless, like a weightlifter. His erection stood at half-mast as he walked to the front of the table and began to massage her upper arms. But Jane was more interested in Perry's erection, which was rigid against his flat belly.

She couldn't help but compare the bodies of the two men, and found that she much preferred

Perry's wide shoulders and the dark hair that high-lighted her favorite parts of his body. He lay with his eyes hooded as the woman's bare breasts passed within inches of his face. The sight spiked Jane's arousal higher, bringing her own breasts to bud just as her masseuse began to gently massage her soft globes.

Having another man touch her while Perry watched did strange things to her. Blood engorged her erogenous zones, and she wondered how long she could endure this kind of torture without an imminent release.

Meanwhile, Perry's masseuse massaged his stomach muscles and all around his groin. Appar-ently his cock was off-limits, but Jane noticed it didn't keep the woman from occasionally brushing against it. The bulb of his erection was scarlet and oozing his arousal. A tiny pang of jealously struck Jane, but was quickly overridden by the satisfac-tion of knowing that this woman might be getting Perry warmed up, but *she* would have the pleasure of his full throttle passion when they were alone.

Jane's masseuse left her breasts pink and erect,

then moved to her stomach and groin, again, not touching her intimately, but coming just shy of it. The man's erection was now as hard as Perry's, but nothing in his touch or gaze made her feel anything but good.

When he moved to her thighs, she parted her legs slightly to allow him better access. He brushed the hair over her mound several times, then finished her lower legs and feet.

Both masseuses re-robed, said a quiet thank-you, and exited the room.

Perry was off the platform and reaching for Jane almost before the door closed. He kissed her hard, squeezing one of her aching breasts. "Let's hurry back to the hotel."

She could only nod, fondling his erection.

He groaned in her ear. "I wanted to be the one touching you."

"And I wanted to be the one touching you."

They skipped showers in the essence of time and redressed as hastily as two teenagers. The cab ride back to the hotel seemed unbearably long, punctuated by discreet squeezes and touches.

They practically fell through the door of her room, and Perry dropped her packages. But when Jane spotted the video camera, she had a reckless thought.

"Perry."

"Uh-hm," he said, nuzzling one of her bare breasts and desperately trying to free the other one.

"Let's make a movie."

He lifted his head. "Hmm?"

"Our own sex tape," she coaxed. "Come on, what do you say?"

His dark, hooded eyes lit with surprise and excitement. "I'm in."

17

PERRY STARED AT Jane's sleeping nude form in the breaking light of dawn, marveling over how familiar and how...necessary she seemed to him after knowing her only a few days.

He glanced at the video camera sitting on the tripod near the end of the bed and shook his head. He'd been so completely wrong about her. Not only was she breathtakingly beautiful, but fun and adventurous, too. And now he regretted that the pact that they'd made had probably kept them from getting to know each other better this weekend. Both of them seemed leery of an emotional attachment, of asking for details about each other's personal life, settling instead for an intense physical connection.

Which *had* led to an emotional attachment, at least on his part.

He just wished he was a little more certain about the future of his firm. He was reluctant to suggest that they keep seeing each other when, in a few days' time, they could be at opposite ends of the earning scale. He had his faults, and perhaps pride was one of them, but he didn't want to be in a position where Jane felt as if he was using her to get to her money.

Like that weasel James guy.

Unreasonable jealousy barbed through his chest.

And the joke was definitely on him yesterday when he'd planned the couple's massage as an exercise to prove that they could have a sexual experience that involved other people. Every time the man's hands had touched Jane in intimate places, he'd fought the urge to drag her out of there.

He swung his legs over the side of the bed. Jealousy was not the emotion of a detached person, he conceded. Then he rubbed his stomach. But maybe it was hunger pangs—they'd barely eaten enough this weekend to keep birds alive, much less two sex-crazed adults.

Regardless, in a few hours, they'd be taking

separate planes back to Atlanta and living next door to each other…at least until Jane moved to a more upscale address. He wasn't sure he could pass her in the parking garage and hallway and act as if this weekend hadn't happened.

But wasn't that what she wanted?

She stirred on her pillow, then her big blue eyes fluttered open. When she saw him, she smiled like a contented cat, a sight that made him want to crawl back in bed with her and give her enough to smile about for the next few days, weeks, and months…

"Good morning," she said, stretching her arms overhead, giving him an eyeful of her perfect breasts.

"Good morning."

She glanced at the clock, then sat up. "You let me oversleep."

"We still have time to pack before checkout."

She laughed. "Speak for yourself. I bought so many clothes that I had to buy a new suitcase to take them home in."

"And they were so completely unnecessary," he said, leaning over to capture a pert nipple between his teeth.

She giggled and swatted at him.

"You seem happy to be going home," he observed.

"No. But I had a fun weekend." She sobered, her blue eyes luminous. "Thank you, Perry."

Tell her. Tell her you don't want this to end.

"I...guess I should go pack," he said, then pushed to his feet and reached for his clothes. "Want to have brunch downstairs before we—" *say goodbye* "—leave?"

She hesitated, then nodded. "Okay. But I can't stay long. My flight leaves two hours before yours."

"Knock on my door when you're ready."

"Okay."

She'd hesitated, he thought as he went back to his own room. Did that mean that she was already pulling away? After all, she had a fortune waiting for her when she returned to Atlanta. A new, exciting life to embark upon, with lots of opportunities to unleash her inner wild child... with other men.

He showered and dressed, feeling anxious and distracted. He had no business worrying about a relationship with Jane when he had so many other things on his plate. But he had the feeling that if he didn't say something now, while they were still in Vegas, that something between them would be changed by the time they got back to Atlanta.

His phone rang just as he finished packing. It was Theresa—on Sunday?

"Hello?" he answered.

"Oh, you *are* alive."

"I'm supposed to be on vacation, remember? What are you doing in the office today?"

"Making sure you're ready for court tomorrow."

His pulse quickened. "Do you have news?"

"Just that you're supposed to be there at ten, sharp. I wanted to make sure you hadn't done something stupid, like get married."

He frowned. "No."

"Just wondering. I've never seen you take off across the country after a girl."

"I'll be home tonight," he said irritably. "I'll see you in the morning." He disconnected the call, trying not to read anything into the fact that the judge was making his ruling earlier than expected.

Or the fact that Theresa had noticed there was

something different about the way he reacted to Jane compared to other women.

A knock sounded on his door and when he opened it, he compared the platinum knockout in long, slim jeans and a figure hugging camisole to the mousy little woman in khakis and ponytail who had knocked on his door only a few days ago.

The transformation was remarkable.

The transformation in *him*, he realized.

"Ready?" she said with a cheerful smile. "I'm famished."

"Me, too," was all he could manage to say.

He hefted his bag and maneuvered her rather large one to the elevator. She carried her small overnight bag and the oversized hard case containing the video camera and tripod. She seemed relaxed and happy, oblivious to his preoccupation. The elevator ride down was silent.

They dropped her large suitcase at the bellman's desk, then were shown to a table in the restaurant.

"What looks good to you?" Jane asked, perusing the menu.

Perry glanced at her, and realized that his

appetite for her overrode everything else. "You," he said simply.

She smiled, but waved him off.

"I'm serious," he said, putting down the menu and picking up her hand. "I've been thinking."

A little frown furrowed her brow. "About?"

"About reconsidering...our agreement."

She set down her menu. "What do you mean?"

He shifted in his chair. "I know we agreed to no strings, but...I'd like to keep seeing you."

Her eyebrows rose.

"Only if you want to," he rushed to say, realizing with dismay that his palms were sweating like a teenager's. "I didn't expect this to happen, Jane, but I think I'm falling for you."

Her lips parted slightly, and her eyes grew huge.

"Are you just going to leave me hanging here?" he asked with a little laugh.

She fidgeted and looked flushed. "Perry...I didn't expect this. I...I don't know what to say."

"Say what you're thinking," he urged.

"Okay." She inhaled deeply, then exhaled. "I think I'm falling for you, too."

Perry's heart lifted and a goofy grin took over his face. He squeezed her hand, then leaned over to plant a hot kiss on her mouth, his mind already leaping ahead to sharing her bed tonight…and sharing the details about things that meant something to him, like the Kendall case.

The sound of someone clearing their throat rent the air, pulling them apart.

A saucy looking waitress stood there, an amused look on her face. "You know this is a hotel, kids. You could get a room."

Perry looked at Jane and they laughed. They placed their orders—suddenly he was ravenous—and asked for the check so they could get to the airport on time. He'd have a couple of hours to kill after Jane left, which would give him time to start making notes about tomorrow's court appearance.

When the waitress left, Jane squeezed his knee, then excused herself and headed toward the ladies' room. He noticed other men's heads turning as she walked by and a fierce proprietary feeling came over him, along with a sense of pride.

She was, after all, going home with him.

He glanced at the hard case that contained the video camera equipment that she'd be checking at the airport, and a worst-case scenario popped into his mind. In the event that the case didn't make it all the way to Atlanta, the camera could be replaced.

But the memory chip…that was another story entirely.

He didn't want movies of Jane circulating the home-made porn Internet circuit. If someone was able to identify her as a lottery winner, she might even be blackmailed.

Opening the case, he lifted the camera and popped out the memory chip, then dropped it into his shirt pocket. Then he sat back and folded his hands behind his head.

His girlfriend was beautiful, kind, smart…and wild enough to suggest that they make a home sex video.

Life was pretty much perfect.

Jane walked into the ladies' room and leaned on the marble counter for support as her knees finally gave way.

Perry had feelings for her...something she never thought—hadn't dared to hope—would happen. She'd convinced herself that she'd developed strong feelings for Perry simply because their incredible physical chemistry was new to her. And she'd been certain that things were one-sided.

She covered her heart with her hand. She was in love!

She hugged herself, fighting back a squeal of pure delight. She had to get out of there, before she did something stupid like write their initials on her napkin. *Just Between Us* had done a show once on how to chase away a man. Number one had been overreacting when he finally admitted his feelings. She could see why women did it—his words had made her positively giddy.

She sighed. Her boyfriend was handsome, successful, smart, and sexy. Life was just about perfect.

Inside her purse, her phone rang. Jane pulled it out, delighted to see Eve's name on the caller ID. She couldn't wait to tell her friend what had happened.

"Hi," she said, smiling into the phone.

"Hi, yourself. Are you still in Vegas?"

"Yes. But my flight leaves in a couple of hours."

"Is your, uh, neighbor still there?"

"Yes. We had such a wonderful weekend! And you're not going to believe this—he told me this morning that he has feelings for me."

"Really?" Eve asked, her voice flat.

Jane frowned. "Really. We're going to keep seeing each other when we get back to Atlanta."

"Oh."

"Eve, is something bothering you?"

Eve sighed. "Okay, don't hate me. But I have some information about Perry Brewer that you should know."

Jane blinked. "You...checked up on him?"

"I was worried about you, so I made some discreet calls. He's an ambulance chaser, Jane. And worse, he's on the brink of financial ruin."

Anger, frustration, and confusion squeezed Jane's chest. "No. That couldn't be."

"It's true. I think you should face the fact that this man is probably after your money."

Jane shook her head. "No. He really cares about me."

"I'm sorry, Jane. But I phoned his office this morning, pretending to be a bill collector. The office manager who answered said that he was expecting a windfall shortly. Then she made a crack about his girlfriend having won the lottery."

Jane's heart stood still. Deep down, hadn't she known it was too good to be true? A man like Perry wouldn't follow her to Las Vegas simply because he felt bad about calling her a homely little geek who'd probably never had a good lay.

Men like that didn't exist.

"I'm glad you had a fun weekend, Jane," Eve said wistfully, "but maybe it's time to cut your losses and walk away."

She lowered the phone. Eve's voice became more distant, then Jane disconnected the call.

Slowly she lifted her gaze to her reflection, except this time all she saw was herself, trying to be someone else. What a fool she'd been. Perry himself had told her that there were all kinds of con men in Vegas who'd try to take advantage of her. And he should know—he was one of them.

The number one con of a con man, she recalled

from a recent episode of Just *Between Us,* was warning his victim of supposed dangers, then presenting himself as the savior,

She'd fallen for it hook, line, and sinker.

Anger and hurt flooded her body. Tears filled her eyes, but she wiped them away angrily, determined not to shed any more tears over what Perry Brewer had said or done.

She stalked back to the table, faltering a bit when he looked up and leveled that killer smile on her. But she was through being played.

"Dig in while it's hot," he said, gesturing to her omelet.

But she didn't sit.

"Is everything okay?" he asked, giving her a look of mock concern.

"Change of plans," she said, her heart squeezing.

"What do you mean?"

"I mean, I'm on to you."

"Huh?"

She inhaled for strength. "My friend looked into your business and found out that you're going under."

He wiped his mouth with his napkin. "That has nothing to do with us."

So it was true. "She talked to your office manager, Perry, posing as a bill collector. The woman told her that everything would be okay, that your *girlfriend* had just won the lottery."

He winced. "That's my fault. I do have a lot of debts at the moment, and I told Theresa to put off the bill collectors until one of my cases is settled. Since she knew I'd followed you, she probably said it as a joke."

He had an answer for everything.

"How does she know about me?"

He wet his lips and looked away, then back. "Because I…did a background check on you."

Despite what she'd said, her eyes watered. "What? Why?"

He lifted his shoulders in a slow shrug. "I was curious, I guess. I can't explain it, but I'm sorry."

Empty words.

"Jane," he said quietly. "I don't need or want your money."

"Excuse me, sir," the waitress said, setting the

bill and his credit card on the table. "I'm sorry, but your credit card was declined."

Jane pursed her mouth and watched Perry go through the motions of pretending to be embarrassed.

"It's on me," she said, digging out cash and handing it to the waitress.

"Jane, don't," he protested. "I have another card."

"It's okay," Jane bit out. "Consider it payment for all the 'tutoring' over the weekend. Thanks. I learned a lot."

Then she picked up her bag and walked out.

18

JANE OPENED HER condo door quietly and checked the hall before stepping out, wearing sunglasses to cover the damage that a night of crying had wrought.

She glanced at Perry's door with contempt, and hurried to lock her door before he could emerge. She'd heard him arrive home last night a couple of hours after she had, had heard him moving around next door, but he hadn't tried to contact her. He hadn't knocked on her door to say he was sorry and try to worm his way back into her bed.

Good thing, too, because she would've slammed the door in his face.

When she got to the parking garage, she noticed idly that his big black SUV was gone. He must have gone into the office early, probably to strategize how he was going to come up with the cash to save his business since his plan to woo the geeky lottery winner had fallen through.

She drove to work, chastising herself—she'd just won over six million dollars, and she was moping around about Perry Brewer. She should be thanking her lucky stars that Eve had had the clarity of mind to question the man's motives in time to stop her from doing something really stupid.

Like fall irrevocably, head over heels in love with him. It was just an infatuation that would fade shortly.

It didn't matter—soon she'd be way too busy trying to figure out how to spend her lottery money to worry about Perry Brewer.

She inhaled and smiled. A new car. A new condo, or a house. Anything she wanted. She had no one to answer to.

And no one to share things with, her mind whispered.

With a sharp pang she realized that from this point on, she'd never know if a man was truly interested in her or in her money. In fact, since she hadn't found anyone to share her life before winning the lottery, it only made sense that any man who was interested in her now, was most likely in it for the cash.

Hadn't both James and Perry taught her that?

A sense of despair crowded her chest—it was an emotional side effect of winning that she hadn't thought about.

She parked in the station parking lot, suddenly self-conscious about her "new" look. She'd pared it down from the weekend, but was still several steps above her normal wardrobe in overlong white slacks, stiletto heels, with a green and blue striped tunic and silver belt. The ponytail was gone—instead she wore her hair long and loose.

People she'd worked with for over three years looked at her and did a double-take when they realized it was her. First came surprise, then the compliments, followed by more surprise. She heard them whispering as she passed. By the time she reached the makeup room, she was nursing a self-conscious nerve rash.

She felt as if she were trying too hard, that she wanted people to notice her, that she was showing off after winning all that money.

Inhaling deeply to calm her mind, she set down her things and headed to Eve's office to field the inevitable questions and to talk about today's show, which was… She checked her calendar, then frowned.

How to Get Over a Bad Boy.

Jane shook her head. Timed that one well, didn't she?

Wishing she'd thought to take an aspirin, she headed toward Eve's office, thinking that they'd soon have to talk about an ending work date. She'd meant what she'd said to Perry about doing something good with her life. Just because he'd faked interest didn't mean that she hadn't been sincere.

On the other hand, she didn't want to leave Eve high and dry at the show. Although, then again, Eve might have plans of her own.

She slowed as she approached Eve's office, frowning at the sound of raised voices. Rounding the corner, she came up short at the sight of the woman standing in Eve's office, arms crossed.

"Liza?" Jane asked, astonished.

From Eve's rigid posture and flushed face, Jane realized she'd interrupted a heated argument.

Liza Skinner spun, her trademark wild hair swirling around her shoulders. "Jane? Oh, my God, is that you?"

"That's what I want to know," Eve murmured, eyeing Jane with shock...and disapproval?

"It's me," Jane said, extending her arms for a hug.

Liza hugged her briefly, but it was clear she'd come to Eve's office with an agenda other than just a reunion.

"Jane just got back from Vegas," Eve offered.

Liza raised her eyebrows. "Did you now? Well, it must agree with you. You look great—like you've been thoroughly laid."

Jane's cheeks flamed, while Eve's mouth turned down at Liza's typical bawdy humor.

"Where have you been?" Jane asked, trying to deflect attention away from herself. "Why didn't you let us know you were safe?"

Liza snorted. "Christ, Jane, you should know by now that I can take care of myself."

"We missed you," Jane added, glancing to Eve for support, but receiving only a sour look in return.

"Right," Liza said dryly. "My job's been filled and the show's going gangbusters. It looks to me as if everyone has pretty much gone on without missing a beat."

"That's not true," Jane said. "We talk about you all the time."

"Oh, *that* I don't doubt." Liza's voice dripped with sarcasm.

"Can't you be nice?" Eve cut in. "You owe us an explanation, Liza, for taking off the way you did."

Liza emitted a bitter laugh. "Why don't we talk about what you two owe *me?*"

Jane glanced at Eve, who seemed equally confused. Eve crossed her arms. "What are you rambling about?"

"My share of thirty-eight million dollars, that's what I'm rambling about."

Jane was speechless, but luckily, Eve had never experienced that affliction.

"*Your* share? Are you out of your mind? We haven't seen you in over a year!"

"I had money left in the lottery pool when I quit," Liza said, looking to Jane for confirmation because she'd always handled the money.

"Not enough to buy tickets for a year," Jane sputtered.

Liza gave a dismissive wave. "We covered for each other lots of times."

"Other people joined the pool after you left," Eve said. "Cole, Zach, and Nicole."

"They each picked numbers," Jane added.

Liza raised her finger. "Ah, but you're still playing one of *my* numbers—thirteen. Don't try to deny it. I saw the winning numbers."

Jane exchanged a glance with Eve. It was true—thirteen was Liza's lucky number. And they had kept playing it for a while after she left out of respect for their friendship. Then it had just become a habit.

Eve pressed her lips together and gave Jane a small shake of her head as if to warn her not to say anything.

But Liza noticed and seized upon the body language with gusto. "See? You know I'm right—you know I deserve a share of that money."

"If the lottery money is the only reason you came back," Eve said evenly, "then we have nothing to talk about."

Liza gave Eve the smirk that Jane knew drove Eve crazy. "Okay, I'm leaving. For now." As she passed Jane, she looked her up and down. "Of all people, I thought the lottery wouldn't change you, Jane. Guess I was wrong."

Jane lifted her chin. "I guess everyone has their secrets."

Liza smiled. "Touché." Then she disappeared down the hallway with a flourish, leaving them once again standing in the wake of Tornado Liza. Jane looked after her, biting her lip. Liza had been stirring up trouble since they were kids, and still seemed hellbent on cloaking herself in controversy. If she wasn't such a creative genius, no one would be able to put up with her.

"Do you believe her nerve?" Eve asked.

Jane sighed. "It's Liza, Eve. What did you expect?"

"Oh, I don't know—a little maturity? A little respect for our friendship? Maybe even an apology for dropping off the face of the Earth? Instead, she plows back into our lives and expects us to give her millions of dollars?"

"Do you think she'll try to…do something?"

Eve scoffed. "Liza's bark has always been worse than her bite, so let's not say anything to the others." She angled her head. "So…how are you?"

Jane blinked rapidly, then nodded. "I'm okay. Thank you for rescuing me."

"I'm sorry," Eve said, touching her arm. "I didn't mean to intrude. I was just concerned." She smiled. "I've never known you to do something so bold."

"Yeah, well…I guess I learned my lesson," Jane murmured. Her inner wild child had turned around and bitten her—hard.

"Did you confront this Brewer guy?"

"Yeah. We were having breakfast. He denied he was after the money, of course, but that became a moot point when the waitress announced that his credit card had been declined."

"Ouch."

Yeah…ouch.

Eve frowned. "Wait a minute—you really like this guy, don't you?"

"Past tense," Jane assured her.

"Well, maybe today's show will help."

Jane gave her friend a playful shove. "Yeah, pretty coincidental."

Eve lifted her hands. "What can I say? I'm here to help." Then she checked her watch. "Speaking of which, I guess we'd better get this show on the road."

After Jane did the guest's makeup—a professed former bad boy who was a little past his prime— she watched the show while she cleaned her tools.

The way to get over a bad boy, it seemed, was to convince yourself that a relationship with a stable, if boring, man was more conducive to a long, happy life.

Jane pursed her mouth. Apparently, toe-curling orgasms and longevity were mutually exclusive.

It was a testament to Eve's professionalism, Jane acknowledged with admiration, that she could pull off a great show even when she was having a bad personal day.

Because despite what Eve had said, Jane knew that Liza's reappearance made her nervous. Their estranged friend was such a loose cannon. And unfortunately, anything Liza did to retaliate would end up reflecting badly on the show.

So, later that day when Eve called her, Cole, Zach, and Nicole into her office, Jane knew something was wrong. With a grim expression Eve passed around individual letters for them that had been couriered over by the lottery commission.

"We have a little problem," Eve announced curtly. "And her name is Liza Skinner."

Cole Crawford made a distasteful noise in his throat. "What does Liza have to do with us winning the lottery?"

"She's contesting it. She insists that she should get an equal share."

"On what grounds?" Zach demanded.

Eve told him about the original arrangement between her, Liza and Jane. "We each chose two numbers to play. When Liza left and the three of you joined, Jane and I gave up one of our two numbers and one of Liza's. Liza says the fact that we were still playing one of her numbers means that we were including her."

"But she didn't put in any money for the winning ticket. Her money ran out a while ago," Nicole exclaimed.

"I know," Eve said. "Don't worry, we'll fight this." She glanced at Jane. "This time, Liza's not going to get away with steamrolling over people to get what she wants."

"So what does this mean?" Jane asked, skimming the multi-page letter of legalese.

"I'm having an attorney take a look at it," Eve said. "But basically, the lottery payout will be held in escrow until the suit is either settled or dropped. Or time runs out and we forfeit winning altogether."

Groans sounded around the room.

Panic flooded Jane's chest—between the hotel, the clothes, the gambling, and the souvenirs, she'd spent over ten thousand dollars in Vegas. She'd expected to pay off those bills within a few days.

Now what was she going to do?

The group disseminated with a distinct cloud of

gloom hanging over their heads, each of them too absorbed in the problems Liza's lawsuit would create in their own lives to offer comfort to anyone else.

Jane drove home in a daze, grateful that she hadn't gone out and bought a new car. When she pulled into the parking garage, she pounded her hand on the steering wheel. What's-her-name's little red sports car was in her parking place, next to Perry's giant SUV.

Furious, she pulled into visitor parking, marched up the stairs to their floor and banged on his door.

The door opened to reveal him standing there in slacks, dress shirt, and tie. Her senses went haywire just being close to him.

"Hi," he said cautiously, his dark eyes questioning.

"Your girlfriend is parked in my spot again," Jane said without preamble. "I'm calling a tow truck in ten minutes."

"I'm sorry," he said. "I didn't realize. I'll have her move it right now."

"Thank you," she said in a clipped tone, then wheeled toward her own door.

"Jane," he called behind her.

She turned back long enough to say, "Perry, you and I have nothing to talk about. Don't even try."

Feeling his heated gaze on her back, she unlocked her condo door and walked inside, flipping on lights out of habit.

Another date night with the television, she thought morosely. Over a salad that she threw together, she perused the complicated letter she'd received today, cursing Liza under her breath, and conceding that she'd love to have an attorney explain it to her in layman's terms.

She turned her head in the direction of the wall she shared with Perry. But before she could fully form and discard the idea of asking him, noises sounded on the other side of the wall.

Sexual noises.

Jane set her jaw. Surely not.

But yes, the noises coming through the wall were definitely of the carnal variety. She sat like a stone, listening to the sound of him making love to someone else. The woman's voice began as a low murmur, but over the next several minutes, her

. noises—screams, actually—increased in volume until she climaxed in a wall-shaking crescendo.

Jane tingled all over—thighs, breasts, stomach—because she no longer had to envision what he was doing to the woman to make her shriek with abandon. She knew firsthand.

She felt wetness on her cheeks, and wiped it away angrily. If she needed any further proof that Perry Brewer was a womanizing jerk, she had it. Was he over there with that woman right now talking about how gullible Jane was and having a good laugh?

Because that was the most humiliating part of it all—the fact that he'd gotten her to admit that she was falling for him.

And now she couldn't even move. She was doomed to have to listen to him have sex whenever the mood struck him.

And while she sat there, apparently the mood struck him again. Jane went to bed early, with one pillow to cry on, and one to hold over her head.

19

"Congratulations," Theresa said, handing Perry a cup of coffee as he came in the front door.

"Thank you," he said, suddenly exhausted now that the adrenaline from the past couple of hours had waned. The judge had ruled in his client's favor Monday, but they'd been made to wait two more torturous days to learn the amount the judge would award for damages.

"So how does it feel to have won the largest medical judgment in Georgia history?" Theresa asked, hands on hips.

"It feels...good," he said, allowing that the enormity of the decision hadn't completely sunk in. Never in his wildest dreams had he imagined the judge would award such an astronomical amount of money to Thomas Kendall. But it was just, considering the man's lifespan had been radically shortened by Deartmond Industries through sheer negligence.

"There you are," Theresa said excitedly, pointing to the television and reaching for the remote control.

"A landmark judgment today in the case of Thomas Kendall versus Deartmond Industries. In his job as a security officer in a guard shack, Kendall was exposed to decades of emissions from the plant's exhaust system. When Kendall developed lung disease and applied for long-term disability, he was fired. Today, a judge ordered Deartmond Industries to pay Kendall three hundred million dollars in damages, and in a rare judicial move, Deartmond will not be allowed to appeal. Kendall's attorney, Perry Brewer explains why."

The camera cut to Perry in the press conference. "The judge believed, as do I, that Deartmond Industries has done everything in their power to drag out this lawsuit in the hopes that Mr. Kendall would succumb to his disease before they could be held accountable. The judge showed great character today when he took steps to ensure that Mr. Kendall will be able to get the medical care he needs to have a reasonable quality of life for his remaining years."

The clip cut back to the reporter. "By the way, an engineer testified that diverting the emissions from Mr. Kendall's guard shack twenty years ago, the time Mr. Kendall first complained, would have cost the company about two hundred dollars.

"And a footnote to this story—Mr. Kendall told me that his attorney, Perry Brewer, is his hero. Mr. Brewer took on the case when no one else would, and has been working nonstop for free for nearly two years in order to get to this historic day."

Theresa smiled wide. "You're a hero."

Perry shook his head. "I'm no hero. I'm just relieved and grateful that it ended as well as it did."

"I'm sorry I doubted you," she said, angling her head.

"You had the right to. I know it's been stressful around here, robbing Peter to pay Paul."

"By the way, did you get things smoothed over with your lottery girlfriend?"

He frowned and rubbed at the pain under his breastbone that ached every time he thought of Jane. "She's not my girlfriend, and no, I'm not sure things can be smoothed over. I pretty much made a mess of things from the get-go."

She gave a little laugh. "I don't believe it. This woman, she's gotten under your skin, hasn't she?"

"It doesn't matter," he said. "I ruined things. Besides, I need to concentrate on getting the firm back on its feet."

Theresa held up a stack of message slips. "Based on the phone calls I fielded today after the news broke, I'd say that you've got your pick of work for the next year or so."

A good feeling to be sure, he conceded. But he still had this nagging sensation of a big, flapping loose end in his life that he'd never be able to tie up. He simply hated the idea of Jane Kurtz thinking that he'd meant to hurt her...both times.

The flash of the Lot O' Bucks lottery insignia on the television caught his attention.

"And now another story about millions of dollars," the news announcer said. "Last week we introduced five coworkers on the locally produced talk show *Just Between Us* who had the winning Lot O' Bucks ticket for a thirty-eight million dollar prize. Monday, a former coworker came forward claiming that she is entitled to an equal share of the money. As a result, the lottery commission has frozen the payout until the dispute can be settled."

"Hmm," Theresa said, shooting him a look. "Sounds like she could use some legal advice."

Perry pulled on his chin, worried for Jane. No doubt she was kicking herself for spending so much money in Vegas. She'd joked that if the lottery money fell through, she'd have to get a second job to pay for everything.

He grimaced, remembering that he'd encouraged her to buy things, to gamble recklessly. Hell, it was his fault in the first place that she'd gone to Sin City.

Perry pushed to his feet and reached for his jacket. He would offer to help Jane. Then he'd get the hell out of her life before he messed up something else.

JANE SET DOWN a bag of groceries to open her condo door. It had been a lousy couple of days—and nights—and according to the attorney that the station had provided for them, things didn't appear to be getting better anytime soon.

Liza, it appeared, had a legitimate case.

And Perry, it appeared, had a legitimate case of the hornies. Last night again, his noisy escapades had driven her to bed early. The only upside was that the yodel-like screams of his partner were now so burned into her brain that they'd almost replaced the memories of *their time* together in Vegas.

The sound of footsteps in the hallway made her hurry. She managed to get the door open just as Perry walked up. He stooped and picked up the bag of groceries then handed them to her.

"Hi," he said tentatively.

"Hi," she said, taking the bag from him.

"Look, this is awkward, but I heard about your lottery payout being challenged."

She didn't respond, just waited.

He cleared his throat. "So, I feel bad about egging you on to spend money, and I wanted to offer you…a loan."

She raised her eyebrows. "A loan?"

"Just until your case is settled."

She shifted her bag of groceries, willing away the visceral response to his nearness. "And how are you going to make me a loan?"

"I won that big case I was working on," he said. "My commission will be…healthy. It's the money I've been banking on to build my firm."

Another con…a loan, in hopes that she'd be grateful enough to let him back into her life—her bed—until the lottery business was settled? "Thanks, but no thanks."

"Jane—"

"Perry," she cut in. "I don't need or want your help. Goodnight." She pushed open the door, then closed it, leaning against it heavily, trying to remember how to get over a bad boy, then cursing because once again, she'd forgotten to buy ear plugs. If she didn't get some sleep soon, Eve would fire her.

She'd fallen back into her old routine at work—chinos, polo shirts, sneakers, and a ponytail. She had officially put her inner wild child on time-out. Her urge to do something bad had had disastrous results.

At times during the day, a snatch of something Perry had said or a look he'd given her would come back to her, triggering a tightening in her breasts and thighs, and she wondered if she'd ever get over him. She had to keep reminding herself that he wasn't the man she wanted him to be. And that their weekend together was simply what she'd gone looking for in the first place…a torrid affair.

She turned on the news while she put away her groceries, but stopped when she heard Perry's name mentioned.

Mesmerized, she sat on the edge of the couch as the reporter described the long, drawn-out case of Thomas Kendall and today's record judgment. Attorney Perry Brewer was described by his client as a hero, nearly sacrificing his firm to work on the case for free.

Jane pulled a couch pillow to her stomach, trying to reconcile the Perry she knew with the man described on television.

His office manager had told Eve that he was expecting a windfall—perhaps she was referring to the Kendall case. Indeed, with a commission from the size of the judgment that he'd gotten for his client, Perry didn't need her lottery money.

Of course, at this point, she might not be getting it, either.

But even if he didn't want her money, that didn't explain why he'd done a background check on her.

Because I was curious…

She worked her mouth from side to side. Regardless, she wasn't going to be just someone he felt sorry for again, like when he'd said those ugly things about her. To him, she'd only been a mercy lay.

Yes, from now on, she was going to keep her distance from Perry Brewer.

From the other side of the wall, the sexual fireworks started up again. Jane laid her head back and groaned. The man was insatiable. And at this point, she had the woman's moans and groans memorized, knew when he did what she liked, knew when they changed positions, knew when the woman had gone beyond the point of control and started screaming her release.

Unbidden, Jane's hot zones began to loosen and lubricate. Now that her body had been introduced to the bone-jarring, mind-bending, hair-curling experience of multiple orgasms, it longed to go back.

On the other side of the wall, the woman sounded utterly satisfied, and Jane tossed the cushion across the room. "That's it!"

She would *not* listen to the man's conquests night after night after night.

Jane shot up and headed to the door, ready to give her neighbor a piece of her mind.

20

JANE POUNDED ON Perry's condo door, her shoulders rigid, steeling herself against the sight of him answering the door half-naked.

But when he opened the door, he was fully dressed in jeans and a T-shirt. "Hi, Jane."

She tamped down a spike of disappointment, then narrowed her eyes. "I'm sorry to interrupt your company, but—"

"I don't have company."

She gave him a dry smile. "Yeah, right."

"I don't."

Jane rolled her eyes. "Perry, I can hear the two of you going at it through the wall."

He leaned on the door frame and a faint smile curved his mouth. "You can?"

Her mouth tightened. "Yes."

"Oh, well, maybe you'd like to come in?"

Her eyes widened and she gaped at him. "How dare you? I'm not interested in joining your... your *party*."

"Really?" His eyes danced. "I remember a foursome that you seemed to enjoy." He paused. "But for the record, Kayla's not here. And she hasn't been since I told her it was over."

Even as she scowled at him, a hot flush climbed her face. "I came to ask you to keep it down. This is the third night in a row that you've been...*entertaining* someone else then and—"

"Keeping track, are you?"

She scowled at him. "It's hard not to, since I can't get any sleep."

"Oh?" He crossed his arms. "Keeping you awake, huh? Why don't you get some earplugs?"

"I...I keep forgetting to buy them."

"Hmm. That makes me think that maybe you *want* to hear what's going on over here. That maybe you like it."

"That's ridiculous—I couldn't care less about your *conquests*."

"All right, that's it," he said, clasping her wrist.

"What are you doing?"

"Introducing you to my latest 'conquest.'"

"What? Are you crazy?" She flailed, resisting him, but it was like trying to stop a tank. He half-dragged her through the entryway and down the hallway into his living room. She vaguely registered the fact that his condo was a mirror image of hers.

Except with leather furniture. And real artwork. And a plasma TV.

"Meet my conquest," Perry said, gesturing to the screen.

She focused, then made a face. "I'd rather not see your porn."

He pursed his mouth. "Jane, it's *our* porn."

Jane squinted. "What?"

"It's the sex tape that *you* suggested we make."

She covered her mouth. "How did you get that?"

"I took the memory chip out of the camera in Vegas."

"You stole the memory chip?"

He frowned. "No! Why do you always think the worst of me?" Then he held up his hands in surrender. "Okay, forget I said that. I removed the memory chip because I was afraid if you left it in the camera when you checked the bag, that it might get stolen and be circulated. I meant to give it to you, but then we argued and I honestly forgot about it."

She hesitated. It was a plausible story, but still... "So you decided to keep it for your personal collection?"

He pressed his lips together, then averted his gaze. "I was planning to give it back."

"Really? When?"

His face darkened with anger. "You can have it now." He pressed a button on the DVD player, removed the unmarked disc and handed it to her.

She wiggled her fingers. "And the memory card?"

Leaning over an external drive sitting next to his computer, he ejected the chip, then pressed it into her palm.

She held up the DVD. "Is this the only copy?"

"Yes."

"Why should I believe you?"

"Because I wouldn't hurt you, not on purpose."

She exhaled slowly—he sounded suspiciously

sincere. But she still didn't trust him. "Goodbye." She walked past him.

"Jane," he said behind her.

She turned and her heart kicked up a beat. His dark hair was hand-ruffled, his shoulders stretching the seams of the T-shirt, his jeans worn in all the right places. He was gorgeous. But her breathing was most compromised by the fact that she knew every inch of skin underneath.

"I really did just want you to have a fun, safe weekend in Vegas," he said. "Sometimes doing something bad is good for the soul." Then he gestured to her clothing. "But I can see that you've gone back to being your old self."

She lifted her chin. "And what's wrong with that?"

"Nothing, except that you're too afraid to trust your own instincts."

His dark gaze was like a laser into the core of her. She wanted to say that her instincts had been to fall in love with him, and how could she trust that? Instead she simply turned and walked out.

It wasn't until after she was back in her condo

that she realized she hadn't congratulated him on his big case.

She sat on the couch staring at the DVD he'd given her, digesting the fact that for the past three nights, he hadn't been making love to what's-her-name...he'd been watching the two of them together.

She hadn't missed the memory chip, because she couldn't bring herself to watch their "footage" after she'd returned home.

Was it good? She wondered. Did she look sexy? Did the camera capture everything as vividly as she'd experienced it?

A sly smile pulled at the corners of her mouth. And how nice to know that she could look at Perry naked any time she wanted to.

Like now.

She walked to the DVD player and carefully inserted the disc, then turned the volume to "mute." She didn't want him to know that she was curious.

When the camera first came on, she was in the bed alone, wearing the clothes she'd worn to the "foursome" massage. Perry was behind the camera, focusing. Then he joined her on the bed and they began kissing, already on a slow burn from their sexy, unconsummated encounter.

Jane touched her lips, the memory of his mouth on hers was so vivid she could almost taste him.

They slowly began to undress each other, and she held her breath as pink and brown skin began to be revealed. They were totally engrossed in each other and indeed, she remembered forgetting that the camera was on.

When her breasts spilled into view, he feasted on them. The sight of his tongue darting out to lick her pink nipples sent shockwaves through her breasts and to her womb.

On the screen she threaded her hands into his hair, pressing his mouth harder against her skin. Then she reached down to clasp his erection and even without sound, she could hear his gasp, remembered it being a hot blast on her skin.

She moved lower and pushed him back to take his length into her mouth. He fisted his hands in the sheets as she moved up and down, massaging him with her hand on the upstroke. He had stopped her, then grinned and flipped her over.

Her thighs tingled because she knew what was coming next. He licked a slow path up her inner thighs, teasing her mercilessly. On the screen her lips moved.

"Please," she murmured aloud, remembering.

"Please what?" he'd asked.

"Please make love to me with your mouth," she whispered in time with her moving lips.

And he had. He spread her knees and buried his head between her thighs, tonguing her until she was sure she would combust from the torture. When her body spasmed on-screen, the couch moved, and she realized her body was jerking with remembered pleasure.

And when her glorious contractions stopped, Perry climbed up her body as if she were his own personal playground. He sheathed himself with a condom, then he held his long, strong body over hers, teasing her with his erection tucked between her thighs. At last he penetrated her in one powerful thrust.

"Oh," she gasped into her fingers.

The muscles in his back and buttocks contracted

for several long seconds, then he began a slow, long glide in and out of her body.

Her hips began to undulate along with the movement on the screen, meeting him stroke for stroke. His rhythm increased gradually, then more quickly as her urging hands ran over his hips.

His face was a mask of restraint as he continued to pound into her. Then her mouth went slack and she dug her nails into his back as another intense climax claimed her.

Jane felt the pleasure ribbon through her body, curling on the ends.

Suddenly his body stilled, then surged forward to sink as deeply into her as possible. At length, he relaxed, falling to her chest, then rolled to her side with his arm around her shoulders.

She was asleep almost immediately, and at first Jane thought that he, too, had fallen asleep. Then she realized that he wasn't asleep—he was watching *her* sleep, while slowly stroking her upper arm.

They lay like that for five minutes, ten. Then Perry placed a long, poignant kiss on her temple and climbed out of bed to turn off the camera.

Jane frowned. That kiss…

She used the remote to rewind the disc and play that part again. She'd been asleep, completely unaware that he'd kissed her. So why had he? He had closed his eyes and pressed his lips against her temple in a lingering, enduring kiss.

She inhaled sharply.

A *loving* kiss…

PERRY LAY on the couch staring at the television, oblivious to what was playing across the screen.

Jane, Jane, Jane.

The woman was in his head, and in his heart. And right now he was going crazy wanting her in his hands.

He groaned, then pushed to his feet and strode toward the door. His pride was long gone where she was concerned—he'd beg if he had to. But she simply had to give him a chance to prove how much he cared about her, how much he wanted her in his life.

He opened his door, then marched over to stand in front of the entrance to her condo. He lifted his hand and hesitated only a split second before knocking.

Seconds passed, then a minute, then two. He knocked again, wondering if she'd already gone to sleep.

He had, after all, been keeping her awake with her own sex tape.

The door swung open and he blinked to see her standing there wearing a towel…and a smile.

"Yes?" she asked, her eyes wide and innocent.

"I, uh, want to talk to you."

"Okay."

"I care about you," he blurted. "And I want us to give this another try. Because even though I botched up some things—a lot of things—I think that we had something special in Vegas."

She didn't say anything, only looked as if she were considering his words. He, on the other hand, was having trouble concentrating on anything other than the towel.

"I don't expect you to believe me," he started.

"I do," she broke in, then looped her arms around his neck. "I do believe you."

His heart soared. "You do?"

She nodded and pulled him inside, then closed the door. "I feel the same way about you."

"You do?"

She nodded. "I'm going to need a shoulder to lean on to get through this lottery mess."

"I have two," he said, nuzzling her neck. "We'll get through it together."

"Congratulations on winning your case," she said, leaning her head back, reveling in his touch. "I'm so proud of you."

"Show me," he said against her hair.

"Can we be bad?" she whispered, then unfastened the towel and let it fall to the ground.

"God, I hope so." He gathered her against him for a full-body kiss. "How did you like our movie?"

"It was okay," she murmured, then grinned wickedly. "For part one."

* * * * *

What secrets will be revealed about
another lottery winner?
Find out next month in
Underneath It All
by Lori Borill available
wherever Harlequin books are sold.

Every Life Has More
Than One Chapter™

Award-winning author Stevi Mittman
delivers another hysterical mystery, featuring
Teddi Bayer, an irrepressible heroine, and
her to-die-for hero, Detective Drew Scoones.
After all, life on Long Island can be murder!

Turn the page for a sneak peek at the warm and
funny fourth book,
WHOSE NUMBER IS UP, ANYWAY?,
in the Teddi Bayer series,
by STEVI MITTMAN.
On sale August 7

"Before redecorating a room, I always advise my clients to empty it of everything but one chair. Then I suggest they move that chair from place to place, sitting in it, until the placement feels right. Trust your instincts when deciding on furniture placement. Your room should "feel right.""

—TipsFromTeddi.com

Gut feelings. You know, that gnawing in the pit of your stomach that warns you that you are about to do the absolute stupidest thing you could do? Something that will ruin life as you know it?

I've got one now, standing at the butcher counter in King Kullen, the grocery store in the same strip mall as L.I. Lanes, the bowling alley cum billiard parlor I'm in the process of redecorating for its "Grand Opening."

I realize being in the wrong supermarket probably doesn't sound exactly dire to you, but you aren't the one buying your father a brisket at a store your mother will somehow know isn't Waldbaum's.

And then, June Bayer isn't your mother.

The woman behind the counter has agreed to go into the freezer to find a brisket for me, since there aren't any in the case. There are packages of pork tenderloin, piles of spare ribs and rolls of sausage, but no briskets.

Warning Number Two, right? I should be so out of here.

But no, I'm still in the same spot when she comes back out, brisketless, her face ashen. She opens her mouth as if she is going to scream, but only a gurgle comes out.

And then she pinballs out from behind the counter, knocking bottles of Peter Luger Steak

Sauce to the floor on her way, now hitting the tower of cans at the end of the prepared foods aisle and sending them sprawling, now making her way down the aisle, careening from side to side as she goes.

Finally, from a distance, I hear her shout, "He's deeeeeeaaaad! Joey's deeeeeaaaad."

My first thought is *You should always trust your gut.*

My second thought is that now, somehow, my mother will know I was in King Kullen. For weeks I will have to hear "What did you expect?" as though whenever you go to King Kullen someone turns up dead. And if the detective investigating the case turns out to be Detective Drew Scoones... well, I'll never hear the end of that from her, either.

She still suspects I murdered the guy who was found dead on my doorstep last Halloween just to get Drew back into my life.

Several people head for the butcher's freezer and I position myself to block them. If there's one thing I've learned from finding people dead—and the guy on my doorstep wasn't the first one—it's that the police get very testy when you mess with their murder scenes.

"You can't go in there until the police get here," I say, stationing myself at the end of the butcher's counter and in front of the Employees Only door, acting as if I'm some sort of authority. "You'll contaminate the evidence if it turns out to be murder."

Shouts and chaos. You'd think I'd know better than to throw the word *murder* around. Cell phones are flipping open and tongues are wagging.

I amend my statement quickly. "Which, of course, it probably isn't. Murder, I mean. People die all the time, and it's not always in hospitals or their own beds, or…" I babble when I'm nervous, and the idea of someone dead on the other side of the freezer door makes me very nervous.

So does the idea of seeing Drew Scoones again. Drew and I have this on-again, off-again sort of thing…that I kind of turned off.

Who knew he'd take it so personally when he tried to get serious and I responded by saying we could talk about *us* tomorrow—and then caught a plane to my parents' condo in Boca the next day? In July. In the middle of a job.

For some crazy reason, he took that to mean that I was avoiding him and the subject of *us*.

That was three months ago. I haven't seen him since.

The manager, who identifies himself and points to his nameplate in case I don't believe him, says he has to go into *his cooler*. "Maybe Joey's not dead," he says. "Maybe he can be saved, and you're letting him die in there. Did you ever think of that?"

In fact, I hadn't. But I had thought that the murderer might try to go back in to make sure his tracks were covered, so I say that I will go in and check.

Which means that the manager and I couple up and go in together while everyone pushes against the doorway to peer in, erasing any chance of finding clean prints on that Employee Only door.

I expect to find carcasses of dead animals hanging from hooks, and maybe Joey hanging from one, too. I think it's going to be very creepy and I steel myself, only to find a rather benign series of shelves with large slabs of meat laid out carefully on them, along with boxes and boxes marked simply Chicken.

Nothing scary here, unless you count the body of a middle-aged man with graying hair sprawled faceup on the floor. His eyes are wide open and unblinking. His shirt is stiff. His pants are stiff. His body is stiff. And his expression, you should forgive the pun—is frozen. Bill-the-manager crosses himself and stands mute while I pronounce the guy dead in a sort of *happy now?* tone.

"We should not be in here," I say, and he nods his head emphatically and helps me push people out of the doorway just in time to hear the police sirens and see the cop cars pull up outside the big store windows.

Bobbie Lyons, my partner in Teddi Bayer Interior Designs (and also my neighbor, my best friend and my private fashion police), and Mark, our carpenter (and my dogsitter, confidant, and ego booster), rush in from next door. They beat the cops by a half step and shout out my name. People point in my direction.

After all the publicity that followed the unfortunate incident during which I shot my ex-husband, Rio Gallo, and then the subsequent murder of my first client—which I solved, I might add—it seems like the whole world, or at least all of Long Island, knows who I am.

Mark asks if I'm all right. (Did I remember to mention that the man is drop-dead-gorgeous-but-a-decade-too-young-for-me-yet-too-old-for-my-daughter-thank-god?) I don't get a chance to answer him because the police are quickly closing in on the store manager and me.

"The woman—" I begin telling the police. Then I have to pause for the manager to fill in her name, which he does: *Fran.*

I continue. "Right. Fran. Fran went into the freezer to get a brisket. A moment later she came out and screamed that Joey was dead. So I'd say she was the one who discovered the body."

"And you are…?" the cop asks me. It comes out a bit like who do I *think* I am, rather than who am I really?

"An innocent bystander," Bobbie, hair perfect,

makeup just right, says, carefully placing her body between the cop and me.

"And she was just leaving," Mark adds. They each take one of my arms.

Fran comes into the inner circle surrounding the cops. In case it isn't obvious from the hairnet and bloodstained white apron with Fran embroidered on it, I explain that she was the butcher who was going for the brisket. Mark and Bobbie take that as a signal that I've done my job and they can now get me out of there. They twist around, with me in the middle, as if we're a Rockettes line, until we are facing away from the butcher counter. They've managed to propel me a few steps toward the exit when disaster—in the form of a Mazda RX7 pulling up at the loading curb—strikes.

Mark's grip on my arm tightens like a vise. "Too late," he says.

Bobbie's expletive is unprintable. "Maybe there's a back door," she suggests, but Mark is right. It's too late.

I've laid my eyes on Detective Scoones. And while my gut is trying to warn me that my heart shouldn't go there, regions farther south are melting at just the sight of him.

"Walk," Bobbie orders me.

And I try to. Really.

Walk, I tell my feet. *Just put one foot in front of the other.*

I can do this because I know, in my heart of hearts, that if Drew Scoones was still interested in me, he'd have gotten in touch with me after I returned from Boca. And he didn't.

Since he's a detective, Drew doesn't have to wear one of those dark blue Nassau County Police uniforms. Instead, he's got on jeans, a tight-fitting T-shirt and a tweedy sports jacket. If you think that sounds good, you should see him. Chiseled features, cleft chin, brown hair that's naturally a little sandy in the front, a smile that…well, that doesn't matter. He isn't smiling now.

He walks up to me, tucks his sunglasses into his breast pocket and looks me over from head to toe.

"Well, if it isn't Miss Cut and Run," he says. "Aren't you supposed to be somewhere in Florida or something?" He looks at Mark accusingly, as if he was covering for me when he told Drew I was gone.

"Detective Scoones?" one of the uniforms says. "The stiff's in the cooler and the woman who found him is over there." He jerks his head in Fran's direction.

Drew continues to stare at me.

You know how when you were young, your mother always told you to wear clean underwear in case you were in an accident? And how, a little farther on, she told you not to go out in hair rollers because you never knew who you might see—or who might see you? And how now your best friend says she wouldn't be caught dead without makeup and suggests you shouldn't either?

Okay, today, *finally,* in my overalls and Converse sneakers, I get it.

I brush my hair out of my eyes. "Well, I'm back," I say. As if he hasn't known my exact whereabouts. The man is a detective, for heaven's sake. "Been back awhile."

Bobbie has watched the exchange and apparently decided she's given Drew all the time he deserves. "And we've got work to do, so…" she says, grabbing my arm and giving Drew a little two-fingered wave goodbye.

As I back up a foot or two, the store manager sees his chance and places himself in front of Drew, trying to get his attention. Maybe what makes Drew such a good detective is his ability to focus.

Only what he's focusing on is me.

"Phone broken? Carrier pigeon died?" he asks me, taking in Fran, the manager, the meat counter and that Employees Only door, all without taking his eyes off me.

Mark tries to break the spell. "We've got work to do there, you've got work to do here, Scoones," Mark says to him, gesturing toward next door. "So it's back to the alley for us."

Drew's lip twitches. "You working the alley now?" he says.

"If you'd like to follow me," Bill-the-manager, clearly exasperated, says to Drew— who doesn't respond. It's as if waiting for my answer is all he has to do.

So, fine. "You knew I was back," I say.

The man has known my whereabouts every hour of the day for as long as I've known him. And my mother's not the only one who won't buy that he "just happened" to answer this particular call. In fact, I'm willing to bet my children's lunch money that he's taken every call within ten miles of my home since the day I got back.

And now he's gotten lucky.

"*You* could have called *me*," I say.

"You're the one who said *tomorrow* for our talk and then flew the coop, chickie," he says. "I figured the ball was in your court."

"Detective?" the uniform says. "There's something you ought to see in here."

Drew gives me a look that amounts to *in or out?*

He could be talking about the investigation, or about our relationship.

Bobbie tries to steer me away. Mark's fists are balled. Drew waits me out, knowing I won't be able to resist what might be a murder investigation.

Finally he turns and heads for the cooler.

And, like a puppy dog, I follow.

Bobbie grabs the back of my shirt and pulls me to a halt.

"I'm just going to show him something," I say, yanking away.

"Yeah," Bobbie says, pointedly looking at the buttons on my blouse. The two at breast level have popped. "That's what I'm afraid of."